ARA

ARANMEN ALL

TOM O'FLAHERTY

BRANDON

First published in 1934

This paperback edition first published in 1991
by Brandon Book Publishers Ltd,
Dingle, Co. Kerry, Ireland.

British Library Cataloguing in Publication Data
O'Flaherty, Tom
    Aranmen All.
    I. Title
    823.912 [F]
    ISBN 0-86322-123-8

This book is published with the financial assistance of the
Arts Council/An Chomhairle Ealaíon, Ireland.

Biographical details courtesy of James Monaghan.

Cover design: The Graphiconies (Ramaioli), Dublin
Cover photograph by kind permission of Bórd Fáilte
Printed by the Guernsey Press, Channel Islands

CONTENTS

ARANMEN ALL

MACKEREL NETS

THE WAVES thundered on the sandy shore of Port Murvey. Eighty men, the crews of twenty-eight curachs sat under the walls waiting for daybreak. They had come to take their mackerel nets which they had set the previous evening. During the night it blew a nor' westerly gale and the seas swelled. It was early in the month of October.

" I bet there isn't a breaker in the bay that won't be white to-day," my uncle said, as he peered through the twilight towards Conamara.

" If the ebb tide gets hold of them, there won't be a net left in Port Murvey to-morrow," my father answered.

The other fishermen nodded.

The dawn came, dull and gray—an unfriendly, desolate dawn it was. As the curtains of night slowly lifted from the sea, tall dark-blue ridges could be seen moving over the water. Those were the waves that rose over the shallow places. Soon, at half-ebb, they would be galloping majestically along with spray-white manes.

To the north-west of the little port, the Rock of Woe's white crest pushed far into the deep places. Directly to the north the Big Breaker, monarch of shallows, half way between Port Murvey and Conamara, looked like the side of Dún Aonghus in motion. To the north-east nearer the shore, the Little Breaker rose to a curl and fell. Soon it would be woolly-white. Long, lazy waves swept in towards the shore and broke on the strand with a mournful roar, like the echo of a cannon fired at sea. It was nearing full tide.

" If the nets are not taken when the current is slack with the changing of the tide, they'll never be taken," my uncle said. My father nodded his head towards his crew. My uncle beckoned to me and to my two cousins—sons of an uncle who had died—to come.

I, being the tallest of the four, crawled under the curach, got my shoulders under the first stand. Two men, one on each side of the prow, lifted the boat with me. When I was straight, holding up the prow, another man got under the rear seat and straightened up. A third shouldered a middle seat, and then this boat, that has been likened when carried in this fashion to a " gigantic beetle on stilts," was walked to the water. A fourth member of the crew followed with the oars on his shoulder. Our curach was the first to be laid on the strand ready for launching. We turned her prow to the surf and put the eight oars on the pins. Several men who had not yet decided to go to sea gathered around our curach. We pushed her out until she was afloat. Then the four of us took our seats. We held our oars poised over the water, ready to start rowing at a signal from the look-out man. Six men held the curach straight in the face of the waves while we waited for a lull. Then the look-out shouted hoarsely : " Stick her out ! Give her the oars ! "

The six men dug their pampootie-clad feet into the sand and pushed the curach quickly towards the sea. Our eight oars struck the water simultaneously. We seemed to be rowing in a pond for a moment, the sea was so smooth. Then the curach rose sharply and almost stood on end, straight as an arrow in a big sea. Down she came on the other side with a crash that set the teeth shaking in our mouths.

As the first sea fell on the strand we rose on another, not as dangerous as the first because we were in deeper water, but bad enough to prove our undoing if the curach's head was turned an inch too far to the right or left.

We rowed, putting our oars far forward and bringing them to a feather with a graceful flourish. My uncle sang joyously in a voice that was everything but melodious. We were now out of danger, in the long lazy swell of the deep water.

As we rowed towards our nets, we could see the prow of another curach rising over the crest of a sea, then disappearing in the trough. Then another curach got safely through the gauntlet of shore breakers.

" The first one is my brother's curach," my uncle said, with a touch of pride. " The one after him is Mícheál Mór O'Dioráin's."

The three most daring skippers leaving Port Murvey were now on the sea, and soon most of the curachs would be out.

We took our markings and shortly we were right over the first pocán. It was attached to the tail end of two pieces of net. Here the water was deep and we had no trouble taking them. The next two pieces were also brought in safely.

Now, we must go right up to the edge of the Big Breaker.

"It should be on the point of full tide," my uncle said. "Unless we have them in before the tide turns, we'll have to use the knife on them. This place will be in foam in a few minutes."

We pulled right up to the pocán. One of my cousins took in the buoy, untied it and tossed it to me. I handed it to my uncle, who placed it in the bow with the other two.

Then my cousin stood on the transom and started to haul in the nets. He had a long sharp knife between his teeth. My uncle and I were on our oars. The four oars were on the pins, stretched along the side of the curach, the blades inside. A third man was stowing the nets.

The Big Breaker was between us and Conamara. My uncle kept his steely blue eyes on the giant ridge of water. We had one net aboard and about half the second when he noticed what looked like a white puff of smoke on the crest of the breaker.

"Give them the knife!" my uncle shouted to the man on the transom. "Cut, cut, cut! Lay the sticks on her! Every man on the oars!"

Quick as a flash the long, sharp knife fell on the cork rope, severing it in two. The meshes tore with a ripping noise as the curach darted ahead, impelled by the sudden, simultaneous stroke of six oars. The foot-rope appeared for a moment on the transom and in the next was severed with one dexterous slash. The knife-man leaped to his seat and now eight oars were bending in a race with the mighty comber that bore down on our stern. It was a race against death.

We turned the curach's head straight towards the strand, the shortest cut in the direction of deep water. The Big Breaker was getting ready to crash all over the shallows. The one following was a forerunner of others, even more dangerous. At the shallowest spot the mighty reef was already white, the moving crest leaving a cloud of spray in its wake.

We strained at the oars, my uncle urging us on. Usually harsh, he was now encouraging us with endearing expressions. We put all our strength into the pull, in such a way that every muscle in the body was in action. We got the last ounce of motion out of every stroke.

" Another minute "—my uncle began. He did

not finish the sentence, for at that moment as if by magic the mighty wave suddenly towered at our stern and seemed to be looking down on us, the slightest suggestion of foam on its crest.

"Dead on the oars!" my uncle hissed. "Hold her steady!" Eight oars were dug into the sea as we kept our eyes straight ahead and held the curach's stern straight in the breaker. Would it break on top of us? We did not even look at one another, let alone speak. We sat like stone idols on the thwarts as if we had become suddenly petrified. We were dumb with horror of the monster wave into whose maw we might be sucked any moment.

Suddenly the transom rose until the curach almost stood straight on her prow. Quickly, but in what seemed an eternity to us, the sea swept by, breaking a few yards ahead. For the moment we were safe, unless another on came right after the first. No! We were safe. We bent to our oars again and soon we were in deep water.

We had five of our six nets. The sixth and one anchor would be lost. Not so bad at all!

By this time the sea was bursting on every shallow in the bay. We lighted our pipes and rowed proudly and contentedly towards the shore.

" We stopped just in time," said the knife-man. " Another moment——— "

" If your knife hadn't got the footrope the first slash, 'tis talking to Peter by now we'd be," said my uncle.

A MORE boastful man than Big Michael never breathed in Aran. To tell the truth it was hard to blame him, for he was as hardy-looking a man as ever stood in pampooties. There was no kind of work an islander ever put a hand to but Big Michael could do as well as anybody else, or maybe better. He was as good on land as he was on sea; in curach battling with the waves, in the garden planting or digging potatoes, building walls or burning kelp, few were his equal, and none his better. But it was his fame for handling horses that he cherished most himself.

It was at the Fair of St. Bartholomew Big Michael bought the black colt. As long as the gift for Gaelic story-telling survives there it will be talked about in Aran. From a man in Casla in Conamara he bought it and it was of the breed of the hard mountainy horses raised on the old territory of the O Flaherties of Iar Connacht. The Aran men like these Conamara horses because they are easy to feed, and surefooted as goats.

17

Eighteen months old the black colt was when Big Michael brought him from Galway. As usual there were many people on the pier at Kilronan when the animal was lifted on a sling out of the steamer. Those who set up for good judges of horseflesh gathered around the colt after the sling was taken off him. They laid hands on his shoulder, on his chest, on his legs. They lifted his hoofs from the ground. They opened his mouth and looked at his teeth. Then they stood off, put their hands in their trousers under their girdles, pressed their lips together and looked wise like experts. Big Michael anxiously awaited the verdict of the knowledgeable men.

Some said the colt was too low in the shoulder, and that when he went down hill with a load of seaweed he'd throw it out over his head. When Big Michael heard this he let a roar of laughter out of him.

"*Míle sgread-mhaidne oraibh*—a thousand screeches of the morning on ye," he said, good-naturedly. "I would'nt care if his shoulder was down to his knees as long as he has a strong rear. Doesn't everybody know that it is up against the hill he'll be going from the shore to my land with loads of seaweed? What do you think of his rear?" he asked, striking the animal's back with a hand the size of a shovel. Everyone there agreed that the colt had the most powerful rear of any young horse ever landed in Aran. So pleased was Big Michael at this testimony to his judgment that he invited the crowd up to Ned Garvey's for a pint.

Big Michael led the procession up the pier, halter wound round his wrist, his two hands in the pockets of his vest. He walked on his pampooties with a catlike tread. The colt followed quietly. When Big Michael reached the publichouse he fastened the halter in the fence. He led the crowd into the publichouse and they all drank enthusiastically in honour of the horse—and at Big Michael's expense. Between drinks they praised the giver of good porter, and dwelt eloquently on his deeds of daring on land and sea. Only one man seemed to resent the honour paid to Big Michael and that was Michael Thady's John, who fancied himself the strongest man in the island after the sixth pint. He made a few disparaging remarks, but got little heed from Big Michael.

Out with Big Michael on the road then, and found half the people of Kilronan gathered around the black colt. They were as interested in the owner as in the horse, for Big Michael hardly ever left Kilronan without causing some excitement. He was the principal excuse for the existence of the R.I.C., and whenever he came into the little town from his village in the middle of the island police leave was cancelled, and the whole force was placed on war footing.

Now the sergeant stood at the barrack gates, while his men stood behind him ready to charge at the first war cry from Big Michael. But the big man was in a good mood and peacefully disposed. He took the halter off the fence, laid his hands on the colt's back and went astride.

No sooner had he the colt between his knees than the animal reared. Michael held on by the mane. Then the animal lowered his head almost to the ground, threw his hind legs into the air, and shot Big Michael out over his ears. The fallen rider held on to the halter for awhile, and was dragged along the road a bit by the colt who took to his heels up the town!

The sight of Big Michael sprawling on the

ground tickled the ribs of the men who had praised him only a few minutes before while enjoying his hospitality in the public-house. They did not give vocal expression to their mirth, but Michael Thady's John, laughed insolently and said : " Now where is your heroism? You the best horseman in Aran! May my soul escape the clutches of the devil if I wouldn't stay on that colt's back and I asleep! "

" You would! " roared Big Michael. " You son of Michael of the little potatoes! Well, I'll put you to sleep in a minute, and I'll do the same thing to any man of your kindred! "

With that Big Michael knocked him down and then lifted him up and threw him over the fence into a garden. He walked along the road after his colt, and as he passed by the barrack gate he trumpeted a challenge to the R.I.C. and the British Army to come out and fight him. Gaining no response to his challenge he quickened his pace after the colt.

Everybody he met told him that no horse ever went back the road as fast as the black colt.

" I never bought a horse that wasn't swift-footed," he would answer.

The colt galloped through the island like the fairy wind until he passed the Well of the Horns, where Old Nick was seen more than once in the disguise of a bull's head. Up hill he was going until now, but from this place west for a distance of two miles there is a level stretch of road which skirts a cliff most of the way. The people of the island said he went so fast that they thought a cyclone was passing by. Finally he tired and when he came to the strand of Port Murvey he stood up and rested. Perhaps the wide open space reminded him of the wastes of Conamara! Big Michael caught his colt and brought him to a small field near Eochaill Fort. The field was called The Great Valley. It was one-quarter of an acre in area and had a ten-foot wall around it. He built the gap strongly and put blackthorn branches and briars on the top of it. That night the black colt was the talk of the island.

The following day was Sunday and one-half of the people of the island were gathered together at Eochaill chapel. They were lying on the grass of the sloping lawns or walking back and forth discussing things while awaiting the arrival of the priest. They came early so they would have plenty of time to talk about the affairs of nations, and speculate on what combination of sea powers could defeat the English, or when would the United States fight England. But to-day the only topic of conversation was Big Michael's colt. Big Michael was prominent among the parishioners. His voice could be heard above the murmurs.

"I put him last night in the Great Valley near the Fort," he said. "The wall is so high that a goat could not climb over it. He was there this morning, and there was not a stir out of him. He was tired enough after yesterday."

The last word was hardly out of his mouth when someone shouted : "There he is coming down the boreen from the fort."

Everybody looked and sure enough there was the colt dashing down the steepest hill in the island at breakneck speed.

Big Michael paled.

"On my soul he's crooked!" he gasped. And well he might be worried. For in Aran with its limestone flags and crags with fissures between sometimes twenty feet deep, a horse that does not stay in the level fields is in constant danger of getting its legs broken ; and the loss of

23

a horse was the severest material loss that could
befall an Aranman.

" He'll destroy his hoofs on those sharp stones,"
one man said.

" He'll break his legs," said another.

The colt came along the road towards the chapel.
at a gallop.

" Stand before him ye pack of devils," shouted
Big Michael.

Several men rose and stopped the animal. The
colt stood stock still for a moment, his head high
and his tail feathered. He snorted. Then he
turned towards the cliff and gathered his legs
together for a spring. But he thought better of it
and turned up the steps to the chapel. To the
south of the church there was a high wall and the
people surrounded him and got him into a corner
and captured him.

Big Michael put him in the same field again
and spancelled him. But he knocked down the
wall with his head and neck and took to the road.
The briars and thorny bushes that were placed
along the walls he pulled off with his teeth. Then
Big Michael put the loop of a rope around his
neck and attached two ropes from it to his fore

feet bringing his head almost to the ground. The colt learned to walk on his hind legs, knock down the top of the gap with his fore feet, and raze the lower part with his back. It was impossible to keep him in any field. Big Michael was obliged to build a stable for him and feed him on hay and potatoes.

"He'll ruin me," Big Mike would say. "I'll have him shod and sell him to some fool of a Galway farmer next year."

The young men of the island were gathered at Colm Rua's forge the day Big Michael was getting his colt shod. Colm was a giant of a man, almost as big as Big Michael. He had powerful hands and arms. He handled a heavy anvil as if it were a spoon, and he could lift it high off the ground with his teeth.

When he looked at the black colt he cocked his head knowingly.

"That's a bad pet," he said. "Unless I am mistaken he's from Martin Colman Tim's stallion in Rosmuc, and if he turns out to be as contrary as his father he'll give you trouble, Michael."

"He is from Martin Colman Tim's stallion," said Big Michael, "and I knew his father's reputation, but his mother was quiet. I am afraid tis after the father he took."

" I'll say another thing," said the smith with a judicial air. " If it is destined that you should tame him, a finer makings of a horse never stood at my forge than him. Nobody will ever sell you a mule for a horse, Michael." The smith hit the colt a terrific blow on the ribs with his fist by way of emphasis.

The smith started making the shoes. Big Michael was on the bellows. When the iron was red hot the smith took it in a pincers and laid it on the anvil while Big Michael beat it with a small sledge. When the shoes were made a dozen men stood around the colt and laid hands on him.

" Now, fair and easy," said the smith. " Don't frighten the animal."

The smith lifted one of his forelegs and put it between his knees. He proceeded to shave the hoof with a knife. The colt reared and tossed the smith aside. Big Michael who was holding on to the colt's head was lifted off the ground. The animal's eyes flashed fire. When he quieted somewhat the smith seized his foreleg again.

" Hold his head down," he advised.

Several men moved towards the animal's neck. The smith was working on the hoof and for awhile the colt was motionless. Then suddenly he buried his teeth in Colm Rua's back.

The smith howled with pain. The men who were holding on to the colt howled with laughter. Big Michael chuckled, and said in Gaelic that the devil the like of that trick he ever saw done. Nobody tendered condolences to the smith. After all it was his business to fight horses and he must expect an occasional setback.

Colm Rua cursed the colt. He cursed Big Michael. He cursed everybody in the vicinity.

"I'll have to go through life now with one buttock," he said, as he retired inside the forge to submit himself to a physical examination. The damage was slight. The heavy woollen flannel woven in Bartley Madden's loom in the village had protected his person from the colt's teeth. The mark of the bite was there, but the skin was not broken. The smith returned to the fray.

"I'll put four shoes on him. My soul but I'll eat them for supper if I don't," he swore.

The colt's lower lip was tied with a rope and the

men swarmed around him. Big Mike held on to the rope. The smith reintroduced himself to his foreleg by hitting him on the ribs with his hammer. The colt replied by standing on his hind legs and bringing his fore feet down where the smith was standing a moment previously.

" By my conscience, the devil is in that animal," the smith swore.

Then an old man by the name of Seáinín Little Anthony spoke. He was hump-backed but it was believed he understood horses better than any man in Aran. He claimed that a horse had a soul.

" Bring him back to the strand at Port Murvey, and run him over the sand," he advised. " This fellow is accustomed to the mountains of Conamara and he is lonely. He does not like the little fields with the high walls around them, and the narrow boreens. He feels the way we'd feel on the great plains of Galway where there are no crags or flags or tall cliffs and no sea to travel over in boats. We'd be lonely and imprisoned on the big plains, like he is here. Take him over to the strand! "

The people listened in awe to the old man with the wistful look on his face.

" There is not a man living could put shoes on him," said the smith.

" Maybe there isn't and maybe there is," said Seáinín. " Anyhow bring him on the strand! "

It was decided to follow Seáinín's advice. The colt followed the halter as quietly as an old horse. The smith and the other men walked behind him, admiring his gait and his carriage. They reached the strand at Port Murvey.

There is more level land around Port Murvey than in the rest of the island. It is sandy soil. It was here the O Flaherties of Conamara landed in their curachs in the fifteenth century, met the O Briens who were then masters of the island, and wiped them out in a great battle at a spot called the Land of the Heads.

On both sides of the little bay of Port Murvey there is a pier. The main road through the island passes the one on the west side where Robert Flaherty had his workshop and he making the big film. Above high water mark there is a waste of sand which is taken away by the islanders to mix with seaweed and pile on the rocks. This is how those nice green fields with the high walls around them come into existence. The supply of sand is constantly replenished by the sharp north winds that blow in from the sea bringing with it the sand that is made by the action of the sea on the limestone boulders on the shore. In the vicinity of the strand there are wide fields and the fences are low.

It was near ebb tide when the colt and the men arrived on the strand, which is about a quarter of a mile in length. The wet sand sank under the feet in places.

The colt was taken on to the strand. He was double haltered. Big Michael swore he'd stay on his back or he and the colt wouldn't leave the strand for a fortnight.

He grasped the colt's mane and leaped on his back. The colt reared, then planted his fore feet on the ground and sent Big Michael flying over his ears. The crowd roared with laughter. Big Michael tried to mount again, but without success. Finally he gave up in disgust.

"*Mo chuid de'n anachain dó*—my share of misfortune to him," he said. "If I had the money I gave for him in my hands this minute I'd be satisfied."

" What did you pay for him? " asked a tall thin, wiry man by the name of George Galvin, who had lately returned from the United States. It was said that he was a cowboy in the western part of America. He owned a few large fields near Port Murvey.

" Ten pounds," Michael answered.

" Let it be a bargain," said the tall man, stretching out his hand.

" It is a bargain," said Big Michael, grasping it.

" I have only half-a-crown in my pocket," said Galvin. " I'll put it as earnest in him."

" I'll take it as it is the custom," said Big Michael; "but the word of your father's son is good enough for me. You are buying this colt with your eyes open and if you are sorry after-wards don't blame me."

Galvin smiled.

" Give me the halter," he said.

He patted the colt on the neck, scratched him between the ears and spoke to him in a soothing tone of voice. Then he leaped lightly on his back and gave him full rein in the direction of the tide. When they reached the tide Galvin turned the colt's head towards the east until he came to the boulders that skirted the sand. Then he turned his head to the long heap of loose sand above high water-mark. The colt ploughed on through this, his legs sinking almost to his belly. Turning west Galvin drove him to the road leading to the pier.

The onlookers gasped as they saw horse and rider making for the pier. There was a drop of fifteen feet to the water level. The colt leaped. Galvin stayed on his back as if glued. The black horse could swim as well as he could run. Soon horse and rider were on the strand. Galvin walked him to the smith.

" Now you can put the shoes on him! " he said. The colt never stirred while being shod.

" What did I tell ye? " said Seáinín Little Anthony.

" That's the biggest wonder I ever saw in my life," said the smith.

" Maybe he'll turn out an honest horse yet," said Big Mike.

" He'll have plenty of room to roam where I'm putting him," said Galvin, as he took him to a wide field near the strand.

Two things he valued Big Michael lost that day; the best colt on the island, and what was worse, his fame for mastering horses.

WHAT the salmon and trout are to the laird, or even to those of " low degree " who can afford to indulge in the sport of catching game fish, the humble rock-fish is to the Aran Islander. Of the many fish that abound—or did abound before foreign steam trawlers ruined the fishing beds—in the seas around Aran, the rock-fish alone calls forth the sporting instincts of the islanders. The bollach, as we call it, runs from six inches to a foot in length. It is reddish brown or light red and speckled, the colour depending on the kind of seaweed that grows in its environment. It sticks close to the rocks and its favourite food is the mussel, but it will indulge in periwinkle or crab.

One day when the seas on the south side of the island were sufficiently calm I decided to go bollach fishing. I got my line ready, made some traces out of horse hair, attached small hooks to them, tied a stone to the end of the line and I was ready—if only I had bait.

I provided myself with a small bag and went

to the shore where I gathered periwinkles and picked up small crabs. This is a dainty combination dish for the bollach.

Seventy fathoms of line I had on my *glionda* and I could fish from the tall cliffs that rise as high as three hundred feet where Dún Aonghus stands to the west of Gort na gCapall and south of Kilmurvey.

I thought to try the low rocks at first, so I made my way to the Worm Hole to the east of Dún Aonghus. There was a low spring tide and I was able to get out to the rocks that are dry only when the sea is calm and the tide is unusually low. I baited my three hooks with periwinkle and little crabs, picked my way gingerly over the rough jagged rock-heads until I stood on the Seal's Rock. The water was eddying round me. I dropped my sinker and waited. It was twenty years since I'd fished from this spot.

I lifted the sinker and dropped it several times to make sure that I had touched bottom. I did not get a bite. I knew that there was a cleft somewhere near the side of the rock, but I did not remember the depth. I had ten fathoms of line in the water. No bite. I was just beginning to give up hope when I felt a weight on the line. I paid out and it slipped down into the cleft.

Hardly was it down when my forefinger began to jerk violently.

" I have you, my boy," I said to myself, and gave the line an upward pull. He was hooked. I started to bring up my fish. As the seaweed grew in long ribbons out of the rock, deep down in the water I bent so that the hooks which were empty, would not catch in it and give the bollach a chance to wriggle off.

Here he was coming through the water, a big speckled fellow with a delicate tracery on his stomach. What a thrill ! I caught pike and trout, catfish and bullheads, rock bass and blue gills in American waters, but bollach fishing has them all beaten.

I unhooked my victim—he was a foot in length —rebaited and dropped my line again. This time I hit the cleft and no sooner had the sinker struck bottom than there was a bite. This time my prey was more wary. He bit and got away, then returned. The first fellow must have been taken by surprise. I expected to hook another every minute, but looking out I saw a big wave

coming and, tossing my line around a jagged piece
of rock, I leaped for safety. The wave covered the
top of the rock a foot deep. I would most likely
have been swept off. The tide was coming in
and I would have to reel my line up and get away.
When the wave receded I returned and hauled in.
I found another large fish on it.

At the risk of getting a good wetting I took
another chance and hooked a third. By now the
rock was covered, so I took myself off to a rock
opposite the Worm Hole. Two more I got there.

When it was half-tide I left and decided to have
a try from a tall cliff. I put my fish on a string and
tossed them on my shoulder. Climbing up to the
rock that overlooks the Worm Hole, I went west
under the magnificent awning of limestone which
shadows that remarkable oblong pool and stains its
waters with indigo. I walked carefully over the
moss-covered, slippery flags until I got out into the
sunlight. Then I climbed the cliff over the Yellow
Rock across the little bay from Dún Aonghus.

Beyond Dún Aonghus I knew a place called the
Rock of Perdition which the best fishermen in
Gort na gCapall used to favour when I was a boy.

There, one stands on the tall cliff, almost as tall

as the one on which Dún Aonghus rests and swings
the line with the sinker at the end of it over his head
several times and when it gains the maximum
momentum it is shot out into a deep hole called
The Cradle. It is a good shot and I wondered if
I could make it.

When I laid my line on the short, hard grass on
top of the cliff and looked down I confess that I
did not feel quite comfortable. The height was
dizzying. However, I unwound my line off the
glionda, baited my hooks, coiled the line neatly
so that it would not foul, gauged the distance to
The Cradle and, holding the line with both hands
near my right ear, swung it in a wide circle.
Round and round I swung it and then let go.
Out flew the sinker. Breathless I watched it
as the line whipped off the grass, coil after coil.
Plump into the middle of The Cradle it went.
I breathed again. Hand and eye were still true.

Hardly had I taken in the slack and sat on the
brink of the cliff with my feet dangling over the
edge when a bollach almost jerked the line out of
my fingers. I started to haul. To save the line
from getting cut by the friction against the limestone rock on the brink of the cliff I pulled it over

37

the toe of my pampootie. I thought it was an unusually heavy bollach, but it wasn't. There were two of them. Well, this was fishing.

I continued, sometimes striking The Cradle, but more often going wide of the mark. When I missed The Cradle I would haul in my line and make another try. It was hard work, but glorious. The view was inspiring. Soft, fleecy clouds floated in a sky of azure blue. The Brandon Mountains could be seen in the distance and the Cliffs of Moher shimmered in the haze. I was too busy with my fishing to wax lyrical over the scene, but no king on his throne ever felt more kingly than I did sitting there on the tall cliffs hauling up my prey from the vast depths.

Fourteen bollach I got from the Rock of Perdition. I tried to make my catch an even twenty, but failed. Tired and hungry, but happy, I plodded home with nineteen rock-fish, " every one of them as heavy as an old bream," as Anthony Patsy Nora Brian, the oldest man in Gort na g Capall, said when I proudly showed him my catch.

And I sat down on a stone with him at the Port of the Fort's Mouth while he told me stories of the fish and the fishermen of his youth.

"WE CALL them big ones," said the old man, pointing to the bollach, "and they are big for that kind of fish, even if they are not as big as the sows of bollach I caught at the Rock of Perdition. But the fish I call big are the giants The O Flaherty of the pictures is going after, only the ones he's catching are but herrings compared to the monster my father and your grandfather brought in here at the Port of the Fort's Mouth long ago, when I was a boy."

He looked up at me, the light of the incurable seanachie gleaming in his eyes. I handed him my plug of tobacco and told him not to spare the knife on it. Protesting that he had a plug of his own, he hacked generous slices off it lest as he put it : " I might be hurting the feelings of your mother's son." He then lighted his pipe and puffed away contentedly, his dancing eyes fixed on where the sun was sinking in the sea.

" It would take good curach-men to take in a great sunfish," I said. " The O Flaherty has a lot of trouble holding them with a pocán."

The old man spat contemptuously.

" The O Flaherty or the cripples of men he has with him could not handle the great beasts of fish that used to come here over beyond the island in my time and in my father's time. Arrah, O son, they were so big that they were afraid to go into the bay for fear they would be stranded."

" Heh, heh, heh," he laughed.

" Sure," I suggested, " you would not call the big men who are working for The O Flaherty cripples. People say that better men were never bred and born on the island, and it is also said that the O Flaherty caught sunfish bigger than any ever caught to north or south of Aran from Bungowla to Iarárainn."

" Now," he expostulated, " don't let anybody hear it said that I gave out that these men are cripples or imitations of men. You can say if you like that you heard it coming out of my mouth that a finer set of men don't live to-day in Aran or any other place. But it is what I am trying to say in my clumsy way that, compared to your grandfather and my father and the strong men of those days, The O Flaherty's men are like children in the cradle. And as for the Líomhán Mór, let you wait until you hear my story."

"One day in the month of April when I was hardly big enough to keep my waist girdle tight on my trouser I was standing like a goat on the highest spot of the inner wall of Dún Aonghus. You never saw a newly-made floor of yellow clay that was smoother than the sea that day. And more than anything else it was what it would put you in mind of, a terrible big smooth flag of limestone rock after a shower of rain and the sun to be shining on it. This was because of the skin that was on the sea and it twinkling as if millions of small lights were spread out on it.

"You would live for ever looking at the beautiful sight and there wasn't a thought of a useful stroke of work in my head on that day as I stood on the fort throwing my eyes all over the south side from the Cliffs of Moher to the Brandon Mountains and out west beyond, where the fairy island rises out of the sea every nine years.

"You will agree that the sight was worth looking at when I tell you that I was on my way to Bungowla for a puppy and you know how a young lad likes a dog. And yet I just stood there looking.

" Suddenly I saw spouts of water going up in the air out to the south-west from the Clochar Mór.

" ' Sea pigs they are,' I said to myself, and I did not give much heed to them, as I had seen them often before and they were no good at all to us, but a lot of harm for they ate our fish. I was right. Sea pigs they were. They came in a row in from the great sea, one after the other, sticking up their heads and then diving, their tails flashing in the sun as they went down. You would liken them to great eels of silver, the way they curled themselves. It was a brave sight sure enough.

" Then it became apparent to me that there was another kind of big fish in near the cliff. At first I could only see a ripple on the surface of the water. Then a fin appeared and then another, and soon all I could see was fins as far as I looked towards the western end of the island.

" I couldn't make out how big they were at first, but I looked down underneath the cliff, and there was one very near in and I could see him as clear in the water as I could see a bollach in that pool there in front of your eyes."

He stopped for a moment to study the effect of

his story on me. I gaped in wonder and said :
" He was big? "

" Big ! Well now, O son, I am moving towards
the graveyard and my best days on this world are a
long way behind me, and for that reason alone it
would hardly behove me to be spouting lies at
you, so may I not live to put a tooth in a bollach
if every one of those sea beasts I saw wasn't as
long as three curachs stretched one after the
other."

The old man laughed exultantly.

" Sure I thought, not knowing any better, that
it was the end of the world was coming, and that
the great monsters of the deep had come to eat us
when the water would have risen over the island.
There used to be people telling us long ago that
some day the islands would be swept away by the
sea and every time there was a great storm from
the south-west we were afraid the water would
come down on us from the Port of the Fort's
Mouth. But let me tell the rest of my story!

" No rabbit ever ran from a dog as fast as I ran
home to tell the news. My soul was in my hands
and my heart in my mouth and I running,
jumping over walls and leaping great scalps and I

thinking that all the monsters in the sea were after me. I did not stop to draw breath until I struck the soles of my two feet on our kitchen floor. My poor mother thought I had seen either a ghost or a lunatic and she asked me what happened. I told her and I half crying.

" ' Musha, O child of little sense,' she said throwing her arms around me—on the right hand side of the Eternal Father may she be—' it is good news you brought us and not bad news if I am not greatly mistaken.' She asked me to tell her more about the monsters.

" When I finished she let a great shout of joy out of herself and said ' As sure as I'm alive the Líomhán Mór is back again.' Not another word did she say but out she went in the yard, got up on the double wall and began shouting, 'Líomhán Mór,' as loud as she could.

" Soon red petticoats were hanging from poles on the gable ends of every house in the village to signal the men working in the fields that the great Líomhán had come. Indeed I saw one woman climb up on the wings of the gable end stand on the comb of the house where her husband could see her. That will show you how great was their welcome for the news I brought. Soon every man, woman and child on the village was running up to the cliffs or getting ready ropes and spears to go after the fish."

" But I never knew that was a sunfish at all," I said, with a view to getting the old man's opinion on the debatable question, whether the animal Robert Flaherty was hunting was sunfish or shark.

He smiled in a superior sort of fashion.

" May God help your wit and may He forgive anybody who invents a name for the fish of the sea that isn't his by rights. The Líomhán Mór is no more a sunfish than I am. The sunfish lies on top of the water in the sun. You'd never see more of the Líomhán Mór out of the water than his fins and the point of his snout if you were looking at him until the eyes melted in your head."

The old man attributed the excitement of the villagers to the fact that the Líomhán Mór had deserted the island for many years with the result that the people had to use inferior oil, extracted from the livers of dogfish, in their lamps instead of the splendid oil drawn from the mighty liver of the sea monster. If they managed now to catch

one Líomhan they would have enough oil out of him
to keep their little muiriní filled for two years.
For this gigantic sea mammoth's liver weighed
five tons, and one hundred barrels of oil each one
as big as a poitín keg could be drawn out of him
according to my old man. And the oil was useful
for other purposes he said.

" It used to be said by the old people when I
was only as big as your fist that no man in the
islands suffered from rheumatism when they had
the oil of the Líomhán Mór to rub on their bodies.
Indeed I wouldn't be in the shape I am in to-day,
O son of my heart, with my head nearly touching
the ground with the hump that is on me, if I had
plenty of Líomhán's oil to rub on myself when I
felt the chill of the cold settling in my bones.
It isn't the hard work we do here that cripples
us, though God knows we earn every bit we put
in our mouths, but it's the poison-cold that goes
through us when we are planting potatoes or
digging them, with the rain pouring down on us,
and our feet without any feeling in our shoes of
raw cow-hide."

For a moment he was aware of his infirmity and
the cloud of melancholy that marked his brow

indicated that he saw the finger of death beckon-
ing to him. His blue eyes were bathed in a mist
and his chin sank on his chest. He was silent and
I turned my head away.

" It is often I get heavy-hearted like this," he
resumed, " when I think of the old days and the
people that used to work and make fun with me.
Ah, the youth is nice ; but isn't it a queer thing
that when we are young we are in a hurry to get
old and when we are old we'd like to be young
again. We'll never be satisfied until we are dead,
I'm thinking.

" But memories of great deeds, will help you to
live your youth all over again," I encouraged.
" Now about the Líomhán? How did they bring
him in with a curach? "

" I have no blame at all to throw on you for
wondering about that, for you saw the lad the
O Flaherty brought in there at Port Murvey and
you know that it would go hard with a curach
crew to bring one of them in on the strand. And
if you believe me when I tell you that they are
no more than sand herrings compared to the
ones I saw, you will say to yourself that the men
of my father's time were men of hero-deeds !

" When the men of the village threw their spades
and their pitchforks in the ditches of the fields
and came home to find out what was on, they held
a council on top of the carcair near your grandfather's house to decide what to do. Your grandfather took the lead of all the men in the village,
since it was his great, great grandfather who first
settled in the village and everybody was related
to him.

" He told the men to bring to the carcair every
rope, slender and stout, and every glionda of
fishing line in the village. He ordered them to
gather all the spears, gaffs, bocáns, pocáns, buoys,
bireógs, straimpíns, long knives and poles and
bring them to the carcair. Then he sent five
strong men to bring all the heavy iron chains
from his little house. The chains were taken
off a ship wrecked at the Big Cleft. Well now,
you'd think with all the noise they made with the
great chains that it was the Old Boy himself was
going through the village.

" It was about dinner time when all the things
for catching the Líomhán Mór were ready.
Your grandfather told the men to get the full of
their mouths of food and to return to the carcair.

" Indeed they were not long eating for they were as excited as if they were going to a wedding, and the young girls of the village put on their brightest shawls and came to the carcair to watch the young men who were putting airs on themselves in front of the girls. Ah, it was great to be young !

" Well, the curach-crews of the village got together—there were ten of them—and by the Deer, they would do your health good to look at them. They picked up heavy pieces of iron and coils of rope like they would lift a feather pillow, and when they walked you'd swear they wouldn't break a hen's egg under their feet. Back to the Port of the Fort's Mouth they went, the whole village following them like they'd be going to a funeral, God between us and harm.

" When they reached the shore your grandfather gave them instructions. He ordered five crews, fifteen men, to put down their curachs and get them ready for sea. Then he told the other fifteen to arrange themselves on the shore, over there to the east of the Port on the Slippery Flags, where the currents of the sea bring in the wrack to the Big Cleft. There, if you notice are great boulders, down in hollows with smooth sides from the constant rolling around of the boulders in them. And so deep are those hollows—you know them as well as I do—and so big are the boulders that one of the Kerry giants who used to throw stones at the giants of Conamara long ago across these islands, could not lift one of them boulders out of a bullán. Yet a child could move one of them with his foot.

" Your grandfather told the men he left on shore to twist the great chains around the largest boulder in the deepest bullán, like you'd twist a súgán on a ball. And to the loose end of the chain he told them to tie the strongest cable, and to the cable the strongest and most dependable rope that ever hauled a cliffman up the Yellow Gable. ' Ye have enough ropes of all kinds to go half way from here to the Brandon Mountains,' he said, ' and if the Líomhán isn't tired out before he gets the chain off the boulder, nothing can stop him.' "

" Your grandfather was a hard stern man, and my skin to the Devil if he could get three words out of him without one of them being a curse, and that day he cursed plenty because he was excited.

But he had knowledge of his business. He chose the best spear of the lot and tied it by the ring to the slender rope.

" ' We are ready for action now,' he said.

" The five curach crews he left ashore went their way to the Slippery Flags where they carried out their orders. The other five crews had their curachs down on the Little Rough Rock.

" Your grandfather, my father and Colm of the Shaggy Beard made one curach crew. By the Strength of the Book they were elegant men on curach stands. They had nothing in their curach when they left the shore, but the one big spear. In the other curachs were the gaffs, bocáns, pocáns, poles, knives and other things that might be needed in the expected battle with the Líomhán. Colm of the Shaggy Beard sat on the transom of the curach holding the spear over his head, the rope in the handle of it reaching the boulder in the bullán.

" I was as proud as if I brought the Líomhán Mór ashore as I stood there on a large stone, looking out at the monsters of fish that swarmed in the mouth of the bay and listening to the women and old men talking about them and saying what a knowledgeable ladeen I was and I only learning from my mother what they were!

" The curachs didn't have far to go but because the women of the village were looking at them, the men stretched themselves on their oars. Men used to go to war for women long ago they say? Ee-ah? "

He waited a moment with quizzical eyes for my comment.

" Ay, I am afraid they have been the cause of a deal of trouble," I assented. " But on your life don't get me started? "

" I ask your excuse," he grinned.

" The Líomháns were as thick as mackerel in the mouth of the bay. They were from the Little Wave to Ryder's Reef, and you wouldn't know which one was bigger than the other. Your grandfather rowed up on one he thought was by himself and signalled the other curachs to stand by for fear of accident. The big monsters did not heed the curachs at all. They were not afraid, for it is said that next to the whale the Líomhán is the biggest fish in the sea.

" Now, it is said, that a whale can pull a big ship under the sea and if that is so, what couldn't this fish do with a curach, any two men can carry on their shoulders. Small wonder then that every woman in the village had her heart in her mouth when the men who were to spear the monster backwatered down on him. One tap of his tail on the curach and the crew would be gone the way of the just. I was young and thoughtless, but I could hear the women praying and saying ' O, Mhuire, Mhuire! '

" Then we saw Colm of the Shaggy Beard who had the spear, stand on the transom seat, his eyes riveted on the Líomhán. The two other members of the crew backwatered smoothly. They came down on the fish so noiselessly that you'd think it was wafted by the wind they were. The other curachs stood by. Then we saw Colm giving the signal to his comrades to hold the curach, and as he did he lifted the spear high in the air and bending down with it drove its head deep into the sea beast. At the same time the four rowing sticks were bent on the curach and she darted away, but not quick enough to clear the wave the wounded monster put from him as he dived to the bottom.

" The curach was hit on the side and over she went. Out with the three men on top of their heads into the sea. The sky was immediately split with the shouts of the other men on sea and shore and the shrieks and wails of the women.

" If I live to be twice as old again, I'll never forget the sight that I saw then. The sea in front of me around the curachs was churned into foam with the tail lashings of the wounded monster, who because of the shallowness of the place, hit the bottom when he dived and so he had to come up again. The other Líomháns were swimming around as if nothing had happened. In between them were three men, going up and down in the water and their black hats floating on the sea near them. The curachs were darting to save the men. The upturned curach looked like a black whale you'd see in the picture books. Everything was gone awry at that moment.

" Luckily the men were saved and when the capsized curach was righted and the oars put on their pins the men went back into her. The Líomhán was going down and coming up in the shallow water, and as much blood came out of him as would come out of a bull. Then he suddenly turned out to sea. The boulder in the bullán started to dance and hop. You never saw

THE LÍOMHÁN MÓR

such a sight in your life. It would jump a foot
off the bottom sometimes. Maybe the monster
would be able to jerk the boulder out of the
hollow! Then chains and ropes and the spear
would be lost, and I would be called a child of
misfortune for seeing the big fish.

" Maybe the rope would break! By the Deer it
didn't. Now the chain was rattling out. Musha
you never heard such a racket in your life as the
chain and the boulder made. Suddenly the boulder
stopped dancing.

" ' Start hauling now,' your grandfather shouted.
' The Líomhán is making for the land.'

" Every man and woman went on the chain and
pulled. There was no weight on it. It was thought
at first that the Líomhán had broken the cable.
But, no! It was how he was half-killed and he
couldn't fight any more. There was enough life
in him to let himself be towed in and when
the full tide went out a bit there he was, high
and dry, stretching on the Slippery Flags, ten
fathoms long. His liver weighed every ounce of
five tons.

" Now, do you think the men of to-day could
bring in a fish like that? "

I told the seanachie that for many weighty reasons I did not wish to give an opinion.

" How did you get the oil out of him? " I asked.

" To boil it in big pots we did," he answered. "Did you see the big iron cauldrons in the meadow near Kilmurvey? It is said that it is out of those pots the giants of olden days used to eat their food. It's in those the livers would be put to boil. My father often told me that he remembered getting as much as fifty pounds for the liver of one Líomhán. And if they had the right kind of boats to catch them they would make a lot of money. Only a few had boats like the ones The O Flaherty is using in the picture.

" And so as I was saying those bollach are no great thing compared to the Líomhán," he finished.

"Maybe not," said I, "but they'll taste better."

JAMES DOOLEY, Rate Collector, was angry. He was angry with Colman Driscoll; but still more angry with Martin Farren.

" I didn't expect anything else from that devil, Colman Driscoll, who is always in court ; but Martin Farren used to be a decent fellow. It's how they all begrudge me this job and I don't know but its them damned Republicans that's putting them up to it," said Dooley to whoever wanted to listen. And indeed everybody was glad to listen and say "H-m-m" and "Now, I don't know faith but maybe there might be some truth in what you are saying, at that." The people were good at listening with impassive faces to the woeful tales of petty officials and retelling them afterwards with gusto.

Martin Farren was standing at the gate of the courthouse. Next to the hall of justice was Ned Garvey's public-house. Martin was debating with himself whether he should have a pint or two of porter to loosen up his stammering tongue for the court ordeal when Colman Driscoll came along.

" We'll clean up that maggoty Dooley to-day, Martin," Coleman greeted. " I'll prove that I'm not obliged to pay until the Revaluation Officer passes judgment on the dispute."

" Bydad I don't know a damn thing about it, but I'd like to get more time to pay," said Farren gloomily.

" Tut, tut, man!" Driscoll snorted. "You're lost if you take up that tack. Go on the offensive, man! Challenge his right to collect from you until you have explored all the byways of the law, and appeal to the higher powers of the land. Follow my line, Martin, and you'll be all right."

" I'd pay if I had the money," Martin said.

" I have the money, and faith the devil a pay I'll do," Colman Driscoll laughed. " And I'll make the judge agree with me. Come and let's have a wet, Martin."

Martin and Colman had a few pints and when they reappeared at the gate the judge was coming up the road from the steamer, accompanied by the rate collector and the police sergeant, one on each side of him.

" Look at them two devils with the gentleman," Colman Driscoll said. " The two bloody parasites. The likes of them are the curse of the country. Only for men like myself, that stand between them and the poor, there wouldn't be any right at all here."

" Devil a word of lie for you in that," said Martin, who had three pints of Colman's porter inside his gansee.

" *Céad fáilte romhat, a dhuin 'uasail*—A hundred welcomes before you, noble sir," greeted Martin Farren as the judge came up. Colman Driscoll put his hand carelessly to his cap, and said, " Good-day, your honour! "

The rate collector and the police sergeant gazed loftily upon the two non-official persons.

" A thousand thanks to you, gentlemen," said the judge, and passed into the courthouse. He was a tall thin man of about fifty years of age, dressed in a suit of Donegal tweed, knee breeches and heavy woollen stockings, and boots that unquestionably bore an Irish trade-mark on their soles.

" Your worship," James Dooley began. But was unceremoniously interrupted.

" Please don't worship me," said the judge sternly. " And furthermore, I would prefer to have the proceedings in Gaelic. Here in the heart of the Gaeltacht 'tis shameful to be conducting legal proceedings in the tongue of our historical enemy! Huh! Pearse's aim was not only an Ireland free but an Ireland Gaelic. Have you ever heard of Pearse? "

James Dooley realising that this question was for him to answer, fondled his walrus moustache.

" You mean the Pearse who had the distillery in Galway . . . "

The judge frowned.

" Go on with the case in whatever language you are articulate in," he rasped.

" Your . . . " Dooley pawed in his brain for a title.

" Make it ' your honour ' " advised the judge coldly.

" Your honour, I have two men here . . . "

" One at a time," the judge said.

" Well your honour, the first defendant I'll call 'ill be Colman Driscoll, who refuses to pay his rates because . . . . "

The judge halted the rate collector.

" Why have you refused to pay your rates, Mr. Driscoll ? " he asked.

Colman squared up to the judge and looked him right in the eyes, a smile of confidence dancing on his countenance. He glanced contemptuously at the rate collector as if to say : " Now there is the bumble bee with a job that I ought to have. Small chance anybody 'ud have to get out of paying his rates if I had the job."

" Your honour, I have refused to pay because I believe I'm over-rated," Colman began.

" You're not the only one who believes that," the judge remarked. " Have you any other reason? "

" I told Mr. Dooley that I stood on firm legal ground in refusing to pay until the Revaluation Officer came and passed judgment on the matter under dispute," said Driscoll, looking at the judge with a shade of hostility in his eyes. " I know the law, your honour! "

" If you knew the law you'd stay away from courts, seeing that you are neither a lawyer nor a judge," his honour observed icily. " You must pay your rates and the costs of this case. Next case."

Colman Driscoll stood for a moment like a poor man who had been informed that his life was

forfeit. He did not know whether to laugh or to
cry, so he decided to compromise and do neither.
He adjourned to Ned Garvey's pub and allowed
the steam roller of justice to roll on in its majestic
way.

" Martin Farren has been given extension of
time several times your honour," said the rate
collector, "and he always has some excuse for
not paying his rates."

Fortified by three pints of porter, Martin Farren
dared to look the judge in the face with his soft,
dreamy, Celtic eyes.

" 'Tis little English I have, your honour," he
said.

" Fine," the judge ejaculated. " I wish there
wasn't a word of the language spoken in Ireland.
You need no excuse for speaking the illustrious
tongue of Geoffrey Keating and Roderick
O Flaherty."

Martin said in Gaelic : " It's how I am not able
to pay, because the times is bad, and there is no
price for what we have to sell, while everything we
want to buy is dearer than ever. Some say if we
gave in to England things would be better, but as
for myself I'd never give in if I starved. But that

has nothing to do with the case. Now, if I have any luck at all with the fishing, I'll pay in three jiffeys. It isn't trying to put them out of what is coming to them I am, your honour, but 'tis a hard world for a struggling man."

The judge beamed on Martin Farren.

" The best Irish I have heard since I started hearing cases in the Gaeltacht," he said. " I think it would be advisable to have a law passed making it compulsory on all officials in the twenty-six counties to transact all their official business in Gaelic. I think it would be a good idea to send the non-Irish speaking members of the Civic Guards here to study the language. I'll bring the matter to the attention of the Government. I also think that it is men like you should be rate collectors in places like this, as you not only have an excellent command of your native tongue, but you have a fine national conception and a clear understanding of the struggle our country is now waging on the economic front. You are given three months to pay your rates, Mr. Farren. The case is dismissed without costs. Next case."

" It was the Irish that done the trick," Martin

Farren said to Colman Driscoll in Ned Garvey's pub several hours later.

" I'm going to bring suit for the removal of that judge," Driscoll swore. " A fellow who knows the law has no show at all before him."

" 'Tis what I'm thinkin'," said Farren, " the less you know about the law, the better off you'll be. Bedam but that's devilish fine porter! "

THERE WAS'NT a stick of furniture in the house. From early morning my father and my sisters had been carrying it to a neighbour's barn. They made a thorough job of it. There were a few sods of turf on the hearth, but the fire was dying out. There was no life in the house, except my mother and I. She stood at the window which gave a view of the road that led to our village. She held me in her arms and she moaned unceasingly. I cried out loud. We were going to be evicted.

Presently we saw helmeted policemen coming around the bend where the road to the village of Gort na gCapall branched off from the highway that runs through Aran from east to west.

"*Tá na cneamhairi a' tíocht*—The villains are coming, little white son," my mother said. " Soon we'll have no house to shelter us."

I cried louder than ever.

I was about three years old at the time. I had not started going to school. But even at this early age certain things got indelibly engraved on my memory.

I remember watching the turn of the road, and recollect the fear that possessed me when I saw the helmets coming around the corner and bobbing as the policemen came along.

With palpitating heart I waited for the appearance of the constabulary on the Tuar Beag, the second nearest hill to our village. I had not long to wait. There they came, up out of the hollow, a great muster of them, led by a sergeant. They were accompanied by three disreputable fellows from the mainland, whose business it was to throw out our furniture, lock and nail the doors after the tenants were evicted. These men were held in general contempt. The police loathed them. For a long time after my first experience with them I did not think they were human beings. They were known to us as " rogees," a local variant of " rogues."

The landscape in front of our house had a dreary aspect this morning. It was in the month of March—and March is a cold, bleak, windy month in Aran. When it is not raining in great blinding sheets, there is a sharp northerly wind blowing over the treeless, limestone flags of the island.

Cloud-shadows chased one another over the bare crags. Once in a while a lowering cloud would shed large drops of rain. Then the sun would emerge and send a cold glare over the glistening grass.

The vegetation was turned brown. The ferns that grew out of the clefts in the rocks were blackened through being beaten against the walls of the deep fissures. They looked like potato stalks with the blight.

From our window we could see patches of newly seaweeded land, the weed red and rich looking; on other patches the seaweed would be white, from the effects of the sun and then the rain.

Horses with loads of seaweed over straddles and side baskets were going through narrow boreens, the horses and drivers invisible, and only the tops of the load to be seen over the high, single-stoned limestone fences, usually six feet high, built to protect the soil in the small patches from the fury of the winter winds. This was the best month of the year for seaweeding. The weather was usually too rough for fishing and when the seas were in turmoil seaweed came ashore.

There were no cattle on the land in front of our village. The cattle fed here in the summer time. Now they were among the rocks and little valleys in the wildest and least fertile parts of the island. One might see an occasional donkey or goat trying to eke out an existence from bites of grass in sheltered spots among the crags ; grass that had hitherto escaped the eyes of other prowling animals.

Gort na gCapall was built on the rim of a semi-circle. The ancestor of mine who founded the village appreciated the value of soil, so he picked the rockiest part of the townland for homesteads. The houses were built close together, thirty homes in all. It was necessary to break the rocks around them in order to make it possible to walk out at night with a fair prospect of saving life and limb. Little gardens grew up alongside the houses, where the rocks were levelled.

The village was built above a small marsh, which we called The Loch. It held some water most of the year. It supplied the villagers with water for washing purposes. We got our drinking water from the little stream close by.

The Loch was right under the carcair. Now, I could hear the tramp of the marching feet coming over the part of the road that was filled in with large boulders. A dull, hollow, evil-omened sound came from it. A few snipe rose from the marshes by the Loch and flew away. Some curlew arose and wheeled in a circle, uttering mournful cries. I was still weeping in my mother's arms when the sergeant entered.

I do not recollect what he said. I know he was a kindly man. I suppose he told my mother that he was sorry to perform this painful duty. Maybe he was too.

I remember the " rogees " with hammer and nails fastening the door that opened to the north, the direction from which the enemy came. The wind being from the north, that door was shut.

Then they quenched the fire on the earth and when this was done my mother moaned as if her heart was being torn out. It had a searing effect on my infant mind. I never got over it. The bitterness born within in me by this act only grew stronger with the passing of years, for I learned soon enough that this was no isolated act of vengeance vented on us, but the common lot of those who got caught between the iron fangs of the world's misfortune, and that the punishment for poverty was not only visited on the parents but even on their little children.

The fire was out now. The coals were crushed into black dust on the hearth, as black as our prospects that wintry morning.

Gently the police sergeant told my mother she would have to go out in the yard. Before she left she whispered a few words in my ear that made me cry for all my lungs were worth. The sergeant turned away his head for a moment. Then he placed a coin in my hand.

I had not noticed my father at all until then. He had lived a rather eventful life and an eviction was only another incident. Indeed this eviction was due to the fact that he took the cause of his fellow-islanders with more sincerity than wisdom, if by wisdom we understand putting one's own material interests ahead of those of the community. He was a Fenian and a Land Leaguer, and most of the time he forgot that he was the father of a large

young family. He was used to police attentions
and accustomed to jails.

I recollect him now standing in the yard in the
midst of a group of neighbours with inscrutable
countenances. They were all dressed in home-
spuns, the predominant colour scheme being
white and blue. Some of them were well bearded
and wore black felt hats. The younger men wore
home-knitted caps. A relative of my father's in
modern, machine-made clothes was standing by
his side. He was his favourite of all his many
relatives and the only one present this morning.

My father was the most unconcerned man in the
little gathering. The police were lined up between
them and the door, but there was no sign of
trouble. The police were not to blame and though
there were islanders enough there to wipe out the
small force of R.I.C. nothing could be gained by
violence. The Gort na gCapall men were not paci-
fists and, indeed, at that very moment there were
many bullets hidden away in the house from which
we were evicted, though this was unknown to me
until a long time afterwards.

The " rogees " were now hammering away at
the door that opened on the south and the sound

fell on my ears like the nailing of a coffin. My mother still held me in her arms. I drew the sympathy of everybody and if I were anything of a play-actor I should consider this as my red-letter day.

I don't know how it happened and I never inquired in later years, the subject was too painful, but suddenly the " rogees " were drawing the nails out of the door. I noticed my father whisper to a man who had the most luxuriant beard and the most powerful frame in the village. He was one of his most reliable men in the Land League struggle. He went by his Christian name Colm, It was in Colm's barn our household goods were. I saw Colm going to his barn and opening the door. He immediately reappeared with a small mountain of furniture on his shoulder.

We entered our home. Soon the kettle was singing merrily on the fire. The next thing I remember was my father and his relative sitting at a table eating hot bread and butter and drinking tea. What they were discussing I do not know, but in all probability my father was dwelling on the necessity for making a clean sweep of land-lordism and of landlords. My mother always expressed the belief that if my father thought of his own affairs a little more and about those of the community a little less, the world would be a much better place to live in. She did not understand that she had fallen in love with and married an incurable rebel and not an ordinary husband. And rebels are easier to fall in love with than to live with.

THE WEAVER'S loom had a great fascination for me. I sat for hours at a time watching our craftsman throw the shuttle, operate the crude machinery with his legs and now and then sprinkle the thread with a home-made lubricant. The odour of this lubricant was not as incense to the nostrils.

Women brought large and small balls of woollen thread to the weaver: white thread for the *báinín* and inside trousers or drawers, black or blue to mix with the white for waistcoats, or vests as we called them; and gray for a Sunday or holiday suit if one was lucky enough to own a gray sheep.

The women usually brought the weaver a present of eggs, butter or fish, and the weaver's wife treated them to tea and tasty buttered pancakes. I always managed to be around on these occasions, as I was very fond of pancakes.

The weaver treated me as he would his own son if he had one, or better I dare say—certainly with more consideration than most sons were treated by their possessors in those days. He gave me some of the worst beatings I ever got, and as far as I can recollect for no reason whatever, except that he believed a beating now and then never did a child any harm. He was a religious man and insisted that I pray in his presence at least once a day. As my mother and my school-teacher also demanded proof of my piety, it could hardly be said that my spiritual upbringing was neglected.

In Aran the boys wore woollen petticoats until they reached what I then considered an advanced age. Every boy looked forward to his first suit of clothes with pleasant anticipation. Every year the weaver insisted that when my mother had the wool ready for his loom she should earmark a piece of gray flannel for a suit for me.

We had one old black sheep and this prolific animal had two lambs every year and sometimes three. Her wool was enough to supply my father's requirements ; but now that I was growing out of the red petticoat stage another black sheep was necessary. Unluckily all the black lambs this sheep produced were males! If I had to wait until she had a female I might be in petticoats for the rest of my life.

Then the weaver decided to do something about it. He decreed that he and my mother and I pray for a black female lamb. Our prayers were answered. Next spring our black sheep had triplets, two black and one white. One of the blacks was a female. Now I wouldn't have to go through life dressed like a woman!

I always helped my mother prepare the wool for the weaver. After it was washed we spread it out on the flags to dry and I stood guard over it. There was no danger of theft as our Aran Islanders are quite honest, but hens might scratch around in it or dogs might sleep on it. Maybe a wind might spring up suddenly and scatter it.

After it was thoroughly dried we teased it into a soft fluffiness. Then it was carded into rolls ready for the spinning wheel. When mother had a number of spindle-fulls spun, I held the spindle while she wound the thread on a ball. Then the great day arrived when we took the balls of thread, *ceirtlíní* we call them, to the weaver.

Customers were constantly pestering the weaver about the work he had promised to deliver them on a certain date. He put the jobs on the loom in the order received. But my mother usually wheedled him into making an exception in her case. On this occasion she had enough gray-black thread to make a suit for me. I hardly left the weaver's house until the work was finished.

Finally, the great roll of white, black, blue-white and gray-brown flannel was deposited in our house. We had more yards of flannel than ever before. There was enough to give a new suit to everybody in the house. But there was more work to do before the flannel was ready for the village tailor. It had to be thickened, washed and dried.

The thickening was done in this manner : A roll of flannel was placed on a smooth plank in a narrow passage, made of boards. Two men or two women sat at each end of the passage and kicked the flannel until it was sufficiently thickened. It was tiresome work, but a *reamhrú* was almost as much of a gala occasion as a christening, and people flocked to the house where the work was being done, and entertained the kickers. This is what they call a *luadh* in the Hebrides.

When the flannel was dried and the family council had decided on their one-year-plan for the clothing industry, the tailor was notified. This individual went from house to house making garments. While he was engaged making clothing in a house it was considered bad form for the adult members of the household to do any but the most necessary work, out of consideration for the tailor, who was more of a guest than a hired man.

Our village tailor was an interesting character. Unlike the weaver he was rather unreliable and not particularly systematic. His erratic business methods were reflected in the garments he turned out. He either made a very good job or a very bad job. He was not a half-way man.

The tailor had an amazingly retentive memory. He had his customers' measurements catalogued in his brain. He took one measurement—and one only. If the customer developed symptoms of elephantiasis or the reverse so much the worse for the customer. The tailor ignored all changes of body or limbs and made the garment in accord with his original measurement. He was held in the utmost contempt by the weaver, who took pride in his profession. The tailor was popular, however, because he was an unfailing fountain of news of doubtful authenticity, and his peculiar way of doing business was a constant source of mirth for the people.

Once while under the influence of poitín he destroyed the makings of a báinín intended for my father. The tailor started to make a báinín out of it but as the poitín got in its work he became confused with the result that one sleeve of the báinín closely resembled the leg of a trousers.

The weaver was terribly worried for fear the tailor would spoil my suit. He suggested to my mother that she have it done by a Kilronan tailor.

" I can't do that," my mother said. " I could never look the poor tailor in the eyes again."

The tailor came to our house, with his little sewing machine, enormous shears, a measuring tape and a piece of chalk. He stood me on a stool. He would call out the number of inches and repeat it three or four times. When he had my measurements taken he spread out the flannel on the table and marked with a chalk the pieces to be cut. Then he cut the cloth with a shears. He sat on the table and then started to sew.

He kept up a running fire of conversation while at his work. He frequented a publichouse on the main road opposite our village. Maggie ———— was the barmaid. He got most of his gossip in this pub. When the accuracy of his information was questioned he would say :

" Doesn't Maggie know better. The man from the east and the west stops there. Yes, indeed, the man from the east and the west stops there. Stops there! Stops there! " And his machine whirred as my first suit began to take form. Finally the tailor called me to his presence. He pointed with his left hand to a pair of trousers and a waistcoat on the table. He shook my hand warmly.

" *Go maire tú go gcaithe tú é agus céad ceann níos fearr ná é*—May you wear and outlive it and a hundred better ones than it," he said. " Now let's try it on you! "

If he had mistaken my measurements for those of somebody else it would be too late now to repair the mistake. With palpitating heart I tried on the trousers. A perfect fit! The vest also was a good fit! my mother was so pleased with me that she kissed me and wept. I was her eleventh child and the only son to live long enough to wear a boy's suit! The tailor was delighted.

" He'll make a better man than his father," he said. " You know, Maggie, that Mike isn't the same man any two years."

My mother smiled. She was a philosopher and believed that at least all tailors—if not all men— were liars.

I went out on the street in my first suit. The boys who had already graduated from the petticoat class adopted a *blasé* attitude towards me. Those who were still in girls' clothes regarded me with envy. But I was sitting on top of the world.

Towards evening I came to my mother and said :
" Mother will you let me milk the cow by myself to-night? Sure I am a man now! "

She looked at me sadly and was silent for a moment.

" The cow wouldn't know you in your new clothes, *a stóir*," she said, "and maybe she wouldn't stand for you. You'll be milking her by yourself time enough. I'm afraid that some day you'll be going far away . . . "

Then she drew me towards her and wept. And somehow, though I was never happier in my life I found myself crying too.

THE KELP BURNERS

I^T WAS a clear, calm evening in the middle of July. The smoke from the peat fires rose almost perpendicularly from the chimneys of the village of Gort na gCapall. Women, usually accompanied by children, were returning from milking their cows. The men of the village were gathering in the boreen after their day's work to smoke their pipes and discuss the affairs of nations. I, a boy of fourteen, was standing in my own doorway. I was not yet old enough to take part in the arguments of the village forum. "I wish I was a man," I said to myself.

Looking towards Conamara I could see the Twelve Bens in a blue mantle of haze. They seemed to beckon to me. My eyes wandered over the limestone crags around me, the deep fissures in the rocks, the jagged cliffs, the little green fields surrounded by high walls and the animals prowling here and there for tufts of grass. I wondered if Conamara was like Aran. I had never seen the mainland except from a distance.

Then there arose into the atmosphere between me and Conamara billows of light smoke floating lazily and vanishing. It was the smoke from a kelp kiln, burning on the White Shore. I longed to see a kelp kiln in action. But I was considered too young to be out at night, and sure there was no fun watching a kelp kiln burning in the day-time! I would ask my mother's permission. She couldn't refuse me anything.

Presently my mother came home with a large can of milk. She noticed my gloomy look and asked me what was the trouble. I did not answer for awhile. Then I told her I would like to go to the White Shore where men from Oatquarter were burning kelp. She was silent for a moment.

" They'll be drinking poitín there, *a stóir*," she said. " And I don't want you to be around where that cursed stuff is."

" But I have the pledge, mother," I answered.

" That's true, O little son," she said. " Your father would be angry with you, I'm afraid."

" He wouldn't if you gave me leave to go," I urged. She smiled and then she wept and she took me in her arms and kissed me, and for a

84

moment I lost all desire to see the kelp fire—
I was so happy. But soon the thirst for
adventure overwhelmed me and I looked appealingly at her.

" The teacher wants me to write an essay about
kelp-making," I said.

" Put down the kettle and we'll make a cup of
tea," she said. " But you mustn't stay late."

It was nearing sunset when I started towards the
White Shore. Birds whistled in the ivy clumps
on the rocks and in the sally gardens. Cows lowed.
Now and then a sheep bleated. Voices of men
echoed from the hollow places in the cliffs. I
walked jauntily along whistling for myself. For
the first time in my life I would be away from
home for the night without a guardian. I was
getting to be a man!

I was happy to the point of ecstasy. I pictured
myself sitting down on a cock of dry seaweed or
on a boulder watching the darting flames and the
waves of thick black smoke that became lighter as
they ascended to the heavens. Perhaps I would
have the privilege of helping to carry the weed to
the kiln. I would be given tea and bread and treated
like a grown-up man. Perhaps I would be praised

and that somebody would say : " *Ní ó'n ngréin ná ó'n ngaoith a thógais é*—It is not from the sun or the wind you took it, O son of Michael ! "

I had a mile and a half of a walk in front of me. As I stepped along I thought of the work involved in making kelp from the time the first wisp was gathered until the burned seaweed was in the hands of the buyer. Whatever money was made out of kelp was certainly paid for with hard labour.

When the islanders gathered seaweed in the winter and spring to manure their potato gardens they saved the long rods on which the red seaweed grew, laid them on the limestone fences to dry, and then put them in cocks. These rods are rich in iodine.

No seaweed was saved for kelp until the potato gardens were manured. The seaweed that was washed ashore this time of the year was not as good quality as what came in at the end of spring and in the early summer. Furthermore it rained almost continuously during those seasons, making it almost impossible to dry the seaweed. And the potato was the mainstay of the island. As the people would say : " *Cothuíonn sé duine 'gus beithíoch*—It nourishes man and beast."

86

Every year about the first of May the Big
Breaker half way between Aran and Conamara
rears its crest and sends mighty waves speeding
towards the shore. All along the bayside of the
island lesser breakers come in its wake, and the
red seaweed that grows on the shallow places is
torn up by the roots and carried to land by
the currents. The best kelp is made from this red
weed if it gets to the shore quickly, and is spread
out to dry before it loses some of the precious
juice in deep sea holes and in the burrows
under the rocks. Seaweed that is washed
ashore on a sandy beach is almost useless for
kelpmaking.

To the shores of boulders and pebbles the men
take their straddled horses, a basket on each side
with ropes made of horsehair attached. High
over the straddle they pile the seaweed and hold
it together with the ropes. And those hard Aran
ponies of the Conamara strain pick their way over
slippery, moss-covered flags, between large
boulders and pebbles that give way under pressure
of hoof, with the sureness of goats among the
crags of a mountain.

The seaweed is spread along the roadside or in

fields near by the shore. When it is thoroughly dried it is put in cocks until burning time.

When there is a spring tide a long ribbony weed of deep-red colour is cut at low water. It is rated next to red weed in iodine content. Sometimes this seaweed is brought up from the bottom by means of long poles, called *croisíní* because of the wooden blade at the end of the pole which gives it the appearance of a cross. Black weed is also used for kelp-making, but is considered much inferior to the red seaweeds.

The sun was setting in the north-west when I reached the White Shore. It was Michael Donal who was burning, or to give him his full birthday title Michael son of Donal, son of Patrick, son of Michael, son of Bartholomew. He was a kinsman of mine so I made bold to ask him if I could help. He smiled and said that he needed a strong man that very minute.

"Do you see that big cock over there?" he said. "Well, get a ladder, climb up on it and start tearing the dry fern off the top of it. Don't hurt yourself, son!"

It was an old cock of seaweed that was there since

the previous autumn, and it was thatched with fern and heather to protect it from the rain.

Up I went on the cock and I began to tear off the thatch. I broke the straw ropes or *súgáin* with which it was tied. Every now and then I stopped to watch the blazing kiln and the men feeding the devouring fire.

The kiln was young and the men were going light with the seaweed. The coffin-like incinerator was twenty feet long, three feet wide and one and a half feet high. A fire was started with turf, sticks and dry fern. Once the seaweed got to burn with a little breeze, a deluge would not drown it.

I was not long working when Michael's two daughters came with bread and tea. Michael called me.

" Come down here, son, and have the full of your mouth," he said in Gaelic, the modest way an Aran Islander has of inviting you to gorge yourself with food.

Seven of us sat on the shore to eat. The bread was buttered while hot. This was a feast for a bishop. There was enough bread and tea to feed twice the number. Anybody who came around while the meal was being eaten was forced to share in the food. Two men were taking care of the kiln. With a fresh breeze, sprung up out of the northwest, it was burning evenly from end to end.

It was pitch dark now a short distance from the kiln. Like ghosts the two men who were feeding the flames would appear out of the gloom with armfuls of seaweed and vanish again. The two girls who brought the meal sat on boulders in the glare of the light and looked intently at the fire. The men paid no attention to them, though they were goodlooking girls. Perhaps they were afraid of irascible old Michael. I looked at them and wondered what they were thinking about. Perhaps they were thinking that part of the price of the kelp would pay their way to America. That was the constant thought in those days. As for me, my ambition at that moment was to grow up in Aran, fish, plant potatoes and make kelp. I was in my glory thinking I was doing a man's share of the work.

I listened eagerly to the conversation of the men. They talked of olden times and of the great kilns of kelp they burned, of going to Kilkerrin on the

mainland to sell it and the adventures they had.
That was the way with Aran Islanders. They had
appropriate stories for every season of the year.
In the mackerel season they told stories of great
hauls of mackerel and the dangers they en-
countered taking the nets, the prices they got for
the fish and their fights with the buyers. It was
the same way when they were engaged manuring,
planting or digging potatoes, killing rock birds in
the high cliffs on the south side of the island,
thatching the houses or going down the cliffs
for wrack.

About two o'clock the horizon on the north-east
lightened and soon crimsoned. The sun was
coming up and I was getting sleepy and felt like
lying down. Michael advised me to go home and
to bed. I told him I would after I saw them rake
the kiln. Michael nodded.

" Go light on her now! " he ordered. " It's
time we gave her the first raking."

Then the men got hold of long iron rods and
stripping to the waist they raked the burnt seaweed in the kiln from end to end and from side to
side. They shouted to each other to work harder
as the sweat poured from their bodies. When the

kelp began to run in a molten mass they stopped and threw more seaweed on the kiln.

The kiln would be burned about twelve o'clock the next night. I would be there if I got my mother's consent. I made for home at a steady trot. When I got to the door I lifted the latch noiselessly hoping nobody would hear me come in. But the dog barked a greeting. I sneaked to bed but I was barely inside the clothes when my mother came, put her hand on my forehead and kissed me. Neither of us spoke. I was soon sound asleep.

When I returned from school the following evening and had dinner I expressed a wish to visit the White Shore, but before I could go I had to change the sheep from one little field to another, a distance of two miles. When I came home to report, my father said that a roaming donkey belonging to Patrick of the Hump was in our crag over the Worm Hole.

I cursed Patrick and his rascally donkey and vowed to beat the poor beast within an inch of his life when I caught up with him. Fortunately, I was not able to carry out my purpose, for when the ass saw me coming he lifted his head and brayed in a most insulting manner, then galloped lightly to the fence, leaped over it and off he went towards the Port of the Fort's Mouth, now and then kicking his heels in the air. My anger vanished and I laughed heartily at the animal's antics, and ever afterwards treated him with kindness no matter how often I caught him in our fields where he used to get after knocking down the walls.

Fearing my father might send me on some other errand if I went home I made straight for the White Shore.

The seaweed was now nearly all burned. The men were tired, worn, dirty and bleary-eyed after the night and the long hot day. It was midnight when they threw the last wisp of straw on the kiln. Then they got out their long iron rakes and repeated the process of the previous night. When they had finished, the kelp ran like molten lead. The men put on their white waistcoats and rested while the kelp was hardening. Then they put flat rocks over it and dry ferns. Soon it would be ready for the buyer. If it did not test well they would only get a poor price for it. Oftentimes they did not get enough to pay the cost of carrying it to the mainland.

93

Twenty-eight years later I was standing in the doorway of my father's house in Gort na gCapall. There was no visible change. Men were sitting in the boreen and women were coming home with cans of milk. Birds were whistling and cows were lowing. There was a crimson glow on the north-western horizon. Everything seemed as it was so long ago. But I was sad and wanted to go away again, away from scenes that reminded me of the dead.

I looked towards the White Shore and again I saw the smoke of a kelp kiln. Almost mechanically I walked down the road and strolled towards the White Shore. Michael son of Edmund was burning the kelp. Michael Donal was long dead. His daughters were in America. His sons died. Of the nine men who stood around the kelp fire twenty-eight years ago only Michael Edmund remained.

Michael Edmund was a whiskery, broadchested man. He had four sons and two daughters, and he had made a great saving of seaweed during the year.

" God bless ye! " I said in Gaelic, as I neared the kiln.

" God and Mary bless you," was the collective answer.

Then Michael came up and shook me warmly by the hand. There were tears in his eyes.

" Many's the person was alive and well when you stood on this shore before who is now in the Haven of the Just," he said. " May the Lord have mercy on their souls." He made the sign of the Cross on his forehead.

" *Is ioma ní is buaine ná an duine*—There's many a thing more lasting than a person," I answered.

He nodded.

" Will you have her burned to-night? " I asked.

"Faith we will not," he answered. "In half an hour's time we'll be going home and into our beds for ourselves."

I expressed astonishment, but he only laughed.

" Before I explain," he said, " O son of Michael, you must have a taste of poitín if you are drinking it, and sure it would be from the sun and wind you came if you didn't."

I assured Michael Edmond that I did not come from the sun or the wind, and had no desire to do violence to the family tradition in the manner of treating poitín. He brought me a glass of mountain dew " enough to wet your lips, son! '

I declared the liquor a credit to Rosmuc and listened.

" There's many a change on things since you left," he said. " You remember how we used to stay up as long as two nights and a day with a large kiln. Every once in a while we got our long iron rods and raked her. We thought she wouldn't be any good unless she was running like boiled tar. Now, faith, we just start throwing in seaweed, nice and easy and devil damn the rake at all we put in her. And here's the best of it. When night comes we leave her there and go home and to bed, and around we come in the morning and start up again. We keep on taking our time until we have the kiln burned."

" And doesn't the kelp run at all now and don't you have to break it up with a sledge? "

" Damn the run, O son. They say it's better to have her in small stones or in powder. We put her all in bags now. In your time there was no respect at all for the kelp that was in the bags. Everything is different now. We don't work as hard as we used to and though there is no money we live better than we ever did. We are eating meat now my boy!"

"How many tons are you going to have, Michael?" I asked.

"Now, O son of Michael, I wouldn't like to say anything rash, but if I don't send five tons over to Kilronan I hope I may not be alive a year from to-day. That kiln is twenty feet long if she is an inch. She is three feet wide and a foot and a half in height. I'll have to burn another one. That's not bad work for a year, and we planted a lot of potatoes. Of course I have the help, God bless them. But even so it's good work and I going on my seventy-five. And only for the bad reports we had all the year about the price I'd have another ton."

"You'll have the price of the turf anyhow, Michael."

"Faith I will and enough to buy five times as much as I need. If she doesn't test six pounds a ton at least may I be stricken dead if I ever make another ton."

"That's a rash threat, Michael," I said.

"Ah sure that's only talk," he laughed. "We have to be saying something. I'd be making kelp if I never got a penny for it through force of habit. *Sé an nádúr agam é.*"

And so I walked home up the shore from Poll na Luinge with the pleasant smell of the burning seaweed in my nostrils and the soothing poteen in my blood. What a great life it was, surely, burning kelp, fishing and planting potatoes in Aran.

WE HAD REACHED the Big Chimney at the Yellow Gable and were ready to descend. The cliff was near three hundred feet high, at this place.

Little Jimmy and I were going to gather eggs of seagulls, puffins, guillemots and cormorants. It was in the afternoon of a glorious day in June, and one would think that all the sea birds in the world were nesting in the cliff at the Yellow Gable. They tore the air with the noise of their screams as they flew back and forth between cliff and sea.

Little Jimmy was one of the most famous cliffmen in Aran, and it was only after much urging that he allowed me to go with him on a birdnesting venture. I was only sixteen.

On the way to the Yellow Gable he told me hair-raising tales of cliff-climbing and the narrow escapes he had from death in his time. He hoped I would be too frightened to go down the cliff after listening to him. And sure enough I was frightened but my pride conquered my fears.

Jimmy tied a rope to a rock, and threw the other end of it out over the cliff.

" We might catch a few guillemots," he explained. " Now we will take off our pampooties. They are too slippery for climbing."

We shed our cow-hide shoes and stood on the short, sharp grass in our stocking feet.

Jimmy was a thin, wiry little man, with large, almost transparent ears, a long hooked nose, large fleshy lips, hard, slender, muscular hands and small feet.

His arms were long and thin, and in general he looked anything but the hardy, fearless piece of humanity who could hold on like a barnacle to the sheer side of the cliffs.

His trouser of blue and white, mostly blue, was tied at the waist with a knitted girdle of red, white and yellow thread with tassels at the end of it dropping elegantly down the right hip.

This is the way the upper part of his body was clothed : next to his skin was a plaid shirt ; outside of this he wore a blue flannel shirt buttoned tightly around the neck. A vest with a white back in it completed his dress. On his head he wore a knitted woollen cap with a little bob on top.

I was dressed in the same fashion except that a light gansey took the place of blue shirt and vest.

Little Jimmy stripped to his plaid shirt and fastened his girdle tightly around his waist. I did likewise.

" Let us go down now in the name of God," he said.

Jimmy led the way and I followed down the Big Chimney. The cliff had split about ten feet from the edge, and as we descended it sloped inland, enabling us to walk down as if we were on a ladder. We went down with our backs to the sea. The descent was easy and as I could not see the sea or the abyss below, there was no fear on me. Then we landed on a large flag about twenty feet from the edge of the cliff. I could not refrain from looking down and the sight terrified me. I would have drawn back then and there but my pride again conquered.

" By dad, you came down like a veteran," Jimmy said, as he stood on the brink of the precipice and coolly surveyed the water two hundred feet below.

I wanted to tell him that I came down bravely enough, but that from now on I would follow him with the eagerness of a doomed man on his way to the gallows. As I cast my eyes downwards a burning sensation began to trouble the pit of my stomach : my mouth was so dry that my lips stuck to my teeth. I told Jimmy that I often felt more comfortable.

" You are just as safe here as you'd be on the side of a house, thatching it," he cheered. " Think of something else and forget where you are. We are going to have a lot of fun soon."

I might as well try to forget the agony of a toothache by thinking of next Christmas. Here I was in the middle of a cliff and I was just as likely as not to get paralysed with fear and fall to my death screaming shamelessly. Well, I would have to go through with it. I could return if I wished. I could climb the chimney without danger. But what would Little Jimmy think of me?

" Watch the way I go down to that little hillock below," he said, pointing to a rock a bit farther out than the rest, " I'll wait there for you."

I lay on my belly on the rock, and watched the human fly descend. He moved carelessly, whistling a plaintive melody as he went. Seagulls, black hags and rock birds of various kinds flew all around us. They were not afraid ; certainly not of the things we were afraid. Perhaps they had their troubles. However, at that moment I would have given all the world to be a bird.

" Come on down! "

Jimmy's command broke in on my thoughts. I half-closed my eyes, turned my back to the deep empty space and hugging the cliff proceeded downwards. I tried to keep my eyes rivetted on the piece of rock in front of me, but I could not resist the temptation to steal an occasional downward glance. It was a cruel journey.

" Ah, by the Deer you are as sure of yourself as a cat," chuckled Little Jimmy, when I reached him. " Now, we'll soon be there. Follow me! "

He took a slanting course downwards with his side towards the cliff. From the sea this place looked as straight and unbroken as the side of a house, but there was plenty of foothold. I was beginning to forget the height. Once I was on the point of leaping down to put an end to my agony of fear, but in another moment I was reasonably composed. Soon we reached a wide smooth rock, and I concluded this was the beginning of the ledge that ran eastward as far as Dún Aonghus.

" Here we are! " Jimmy said.

In this place the awning was almost six feet high at intervals so that we were able to progress a little way standing up. In some spots the ledge was several feet wide. Bird droppings were everywhere in abundance. Here and there a dead young bird. Some eggs. Birds of many kinds screamed around us as we proceeded.

Now we had to crawl on our bellies. The odour was anything but pleasing. The edge narrowed to about three feet. We accomplished the distance in safety. I suddenly thought of the return trip. A cold sweat broke out over me. That almost irresistible urge to jump and get it all over assailed me again.

We were now crawling over a rough jagged rock. My knees hurt. I noticed Jimmy sliding over a slippery spot. There was a green moss on the flag, nourished by the drops of fresh water that trickled from the rocks above. A large cormorant scampered by. Jimmy's right hand darted out and caught the bird by the leg. In stretching out his hand he slid and almost went over. Fortunately, his left hand gripped a piece of jagged rock. The bird was screaming and flapping its wings furiously. Jimmy would not let go his hold.

" Let go the bird! " I shouted. " Or it will pull you out."

He did not reply, but held on grimly as the cormorant whipped him with its wings. I expected to see him vanish over the cliff any minute. For a moment I thought my mind was giving way. I laughed and closed my eyes. I saw Jimmy flying over the sea holding on to the cormorant's leg, and he waving me good-bye. But the horrible reality struck me with greater force than before when the slight dizziness passed. If Jimmy went over the cliff how could I find my way back. I could not turn where I was and I had no idea what kind of place was ahead of me!

Again I shouted to Little Jimmy to let the bird go. I screamed hysterically. The man seemed to be glued to the cormorant. If I could catch the bird by the wing I might be able to kill the cormorant and save Little Jimmy. I could not pass between him and the cliff. What was I to do? Again, I urged him to loose his hold, but I only had a muttered and unintelligible reply.

I looked around for inspiration. If I had a *starán* to hold on to with my left hand I might be able to reach over Jimmy and catch the bird. Yes, there was a jagged piece of rock that would give a good hold, but it was on a line with the middle of my body, and I stretched flat on the passage. I had it! I would take off my new, many-coloured, strong, knitted girdle of wool, tie one end of it to Jimmy's legs and the other end to the *starán*. Then I would lean over the little cliffman without danger of pushing him over and get hold of the bird.

I told Jimmy what I was going to do. When I had his legs tied to the cliff I crawled up on him, and when the cormorant flapped his wings again against his body I managed to grasp one of the wings. Gritting my teeth I pulled. Jimmy also pulled on the leg. The odds were against the cormorant now. Slowly he gave way. I reached out and got my hand on his neck. I squeezed the breath out of his body.

" We got him at the last! " Jimmy chuckled. " You'll make a great cliffman! "

While engaged in this task I had forgotten about the peril of the situation I was in, but now that I had time to think I began to get fidgety. Jimmy was as cool after the experience as if he'd not been in imminent danger of death. I kept my thoughts to myself. I knew that I stood high in Jimmy's

estimation—and that was something worth
agonizing for.

Leaving the bird, Jimmy pushed ahead, I trailing
behind. Soon he turned a corner and we were on
a broad flag where the ceiling was high enough to
enable us to stand. Large boulders held up the
rock overhead.

" Here's where the eggs are, my boy," Jimmy
said, looking around.

I shouted with excitement. I never saw so many
birds' eggs in my life. They were for the most
part the eggs of guillemots and puffins, but here
and there were seagulls' eggs and those of the
cormorant. The eggs were varied in colour and
the markings most beautiful. Jimmy made no
comment on the beauty of the eggs. He took off
his cap and proceeded to fill it. I did the same.
When we had as many as our caps could hold we
sat down on the rock. Jimmy lighted his pipe and
puffed contentedly, looking out at the sea. Birds
flew up to their nesting place and returned to the
water screaming when they saw the two thieves
in their home.

" It's too bad to have to steal their eggs,"
I said.

" They won't miss them," he answered. " The guillemot brings up only one young each year, and it'll keep on laying eggs until it gets that bird. It hatches it standing up, and you'll see the little hollow near its tail where it stands over the egg. Queer bird it is. Now, we'll be going back the way we came ; but some night we'll stay here and kill a lot of birds. Only thing you have to do is to bring along a candle and light it. The birds come to the flame and then you have only to stretch out your hand and kill them."

I had doubts about ever coming this way again, and it was with a palpitating heart I followed Jimmy, each of us with a cap full of eggs in his teeth. On the way Jimmy picked up the cormorant.

" He'll make a good meal for my dog," he said.

Now that I had the precious eggs, the danger of the return journey was forgotten. I pictured myself strolling carelessly through the village with Little Jimmy, the famous cliffman, with the spoil of my hazardous climb. And when I called to mind the feast we'd have on the eggs, I was so impatient to get home that I darted up the cliff like a spider.

When we came to where the rope was hanging Jimmy tied the cormorant to it. We got to the top of the cliff and hauled up the lone bird.

" No animal is as mischievous as man," Little Jimmy remarked, looking with eyes of pity on the graceful form of the cormorant. Then he grabbed it by the neck and slung it on his shoulder.

WRACK

THE WIND roared down the chimney. It was ten o'clock at night and the villagers who gathered every evening in our house to pass the time telling stories and discussing various subjects of interest were saying that it was time to be going home. My mother was telling them that it was early yet, but my father glanced significantly at his rosary beads that were hanging on a nail over the fireplace. It was about the middle of January, and when the people were not engaged seaweeding there was little work to be done. There would be plenty of seaweed after this storm, that had raged since early morning.

" I never saw such a sea in the Port of the Fort's Mouth," said the Widow's John. "The waves were coming up on the green grass at the full of the spring tide."

" She'll break through sometime," said Black Coleman. " It is in the prophecies."

My father said "Huh," and relapsed into silence.

" It's through the Blind Sound she'll break," somebody else said.

Then a great blast of wind shook the rafters. A piece of soot fell in the ashes. Our dog Oscar who had his fore paws on the hearth and his nose between them sneezed and looked irritated. There was a knock at the door, then the latch lifted and in limped the tailor.

" God in the house," he greeted.

" God and Mary to you," my mother answered.

" This is a nice time of the night to come visiting," he said. " But I thought ye'd like to know that there were planks and barrels seen this evening off the western end of the island."

The visitors jumped to their feet. In this treeless, peatless island the cry of wrack had an effect on the imagination like the cry of gold in countries where men risked death for the precious metal. The men went off one by one. My father pulled down the ladder off the turf loft.

" Throw down the thirty-fathom cable," he said to me.

I ran nimbly up the rungs of the ladder and threw down the warp.

My father examined every inch of it to satisfy

himself that it was sound. It would shortly be used lowering men down the tall cliffs to gather wrack and hauling wrack and men up to the top.

"Tailor," my father asked, "did you notice any straw flying about? I'm afraid there's a weak spot in the thatch on our little house."

"Your little house is right enough," the tailor said; "but," here he laughed convulsively, "there's a big stripe torn off Bartley Pat's house." Bartley Pat was the laziest man in Aran and also the healthiest.

"It's a shame to be laughing at the poor man because there is as much of the misfortune on him as to be lazy," my mother said.

Then she bent over the stocking she was knitting and laughed till the tears came from her eyes.

"But for God's mercy that man would not have a bite to put in his mouth," the tailor said.

"As long as he's not too lazy to eat, he'll not die of the hunger," my mother said.

"Sure only for the poor man we'd have nobody to make fun of."

"There isn't a man in the village I'd rather have with me in fight or gathering wrack than Bartley

Pat," my father said. "There' isn't enough excitement in the ordinary work of the place for him. Tis a great soldier or a sea captain he would make. I bet he's putting himself in danger of death this minute peering out from the tops of the cliffs for a sight of wrack." Then to me : " Go out and see if the súgáns are holding down the thatch on the little house."

I went out in the yard. Ducks and geese with their heads under their wings were lying in the shelter of the house. Clouds raced madly across the face of the moon. Their shadows raced across the bare limestone flags. A light salt spray from the sea fell over the village. Flecks of foam floated in the air. Groups of men speaking in whispers could be seen making their way to the Port of the Fort's Mouth. Every one of the sixty strong men in the village would be risking their lives for the precious timber by morning. I reported to my father that the thatch was holding.

" Time for saying the rosary," he said.

" Good night to ye," said the tailor, and he left. My father laughed sardonically.

" It never failed yet," he commented, glancing at the door.

The rosary over, my father hung his beads on the nail and took off his shoes. He was going to bed! My heart sank. I expected he would take me along on the great adventure. I looked appealingly to my mother.

" The whole village is over at the Port of the Fort's Mouth by now," she said.

" They are the imbeciles," he replied. " Sure it won't be half ebb until seven o'clock in the morning! "

He went to bed and soon was sleeping soundly.

" Your father knows everything about the sea and the land, *a stóir*," my mother said to me. " Now that they are all in bed we'll make a little cupeen of tea."

This was a habit with us. To-night it was a heavenly treat, a turf fire blazing on the hearth, the kettle singing on the fire, the wind roaring down the chimney and whistling through the stone walls, the dull roar of the waves forcing the air out of the caves along the tall cliffs. Our dog Oscar with one ear cocked was watching the cups and saucers and bread being laid on a low stool by the hearth.

As usual, when the tea was made, we discussed

whether we should wake my father and ask him to have a cup of tea and, as usual, we did. I brought him the tea.

" The storm is weakening," he said. " Go to bed, you'll have to be getting up early."

" He's going to take me with him," I said to my mother.

" I knew he would, little son," she said.

I was awakened by a sharp rap on the window.

" Who's there? " my father asked in a voice just as sharp.

" I," answered the voice of Bartley Pat.

My father jumped out of bed, pulled on his trousers, walked barefoot to the kitchen door and let Bartley in. I heard a murmur of voices. My father returned to the room.

" Be up quick," he ordered. " The sea is mantled with timber. You could walk with dry feet on planks from Dún Aonghus to the Worm Hole! "

He muttered a " Hoh " of satisfaction several times as he dressed. I could see a gleam of anticipation in his blue gray eyes. His voice had an unusual softness.

" Hurry and put down the kettle," he said.

Bartley Pat was a short, wiry little man with an olive complexion. His hair was black and curly, his lips were red and thick. Probably he had in him the blood of some Spaniard whose ancestor had been to the West Indies with Columbus. Though in practice he took life easy there was a worried look in his eyes as if he was not contented in his mind. When going through the motions of working on the farm, he looked like a chronic rheumatic and his clothes always seemed to be on the point of falling off him. But now as he stood on the floor fondling the thirty-foot warp he was a changed man.

His girdle of multicoloured woollen thread was coiled around his suspenderless homespun trouser. His waistcoat was tightly buttoned over his blue shirt, and his báinín neatly tucked under his girdle. On his feet was a pair of new pampooties, the hair cut off and the cords with which they were laced over his feet correctly knotted over the thick woollen stockings. He was crowned with a blue, knit woollen cap. From head to heel Bartley was clothed in Aran wool, carded, spun, woven, thickened and tailored in the village of Gort na gCapall !

As Bartley fingered the rope to make sure there were no flaws in it he expressed his satisfaction by saying " Heh! "

" Soon I'll be going down the cliff at the Blind Sound at the end of this," he said to me proudly.

I set about raking up the fire. It did not take long as my mother before she went to bed had made a heap of large coals on the hearth, and blanketed them with ashes so that they did not burn. Outside the ashes she laid several sods of turf. These were so dry that they burst into flame when I piled them over and around the hot coals and blew on them.

I had the kettle on the fire and the teapot warming on the hearth when my father appeared. He looked at me and nodded approvingly. He then addressed Bartley :

" Who else is coming? "

" Little Jimmy, the son of Dick Shameen's Michael, the Widow's John and Patrick and Black Colm. Some of them are watching on the cliff now and picking out a good spot for going down.

" Hah! " my father said. " Of course we're

starting at the Blind Sound ! To-morrow will be
time enough for the Cliff of the Limpets."

" Yes, the wind being coming down straight on
the land, the wrack was thrown into the first large
bay from the west of the island. There is a long
stretch of strand at the Blind Sound when the
tide is at low ebb."

My father nodded.

" You'll be needing two men below with you? "
he asked.

" That will be enough. I'll take Black Colm, and
the Widow's John."

My father nodded again.

" The choice is yours," he said. " The storm
has weakened. Is the sea falling? "

" She couldn't rise any higher."

Little Jimmy and Black Colm came in. My
mother got up and welcomed the villagers. She
produced a bowl of eggs from the dresser and put
several of them in a large saucepan. With one
voice the villagers protested they did not want any
eggs.

" Arrah, whisht ye! " said my mother. " Ye'll
want something to keep the soul in ye. Sure
there is no strength at all in that tea." She

laid a print of butter on the table while I made the tea. It was a feast!

My father sat at the head of the table and ate without haste. When one of the men suggested they be getting on towards the cliff he observed that the proper respect should be paid to food, and that nobody should leave the table in haste. This point of view prevailed, and none of us got up until all the eggs were devoured except one. The lone egg was a sacrifice to the simple table code of the Aran Islands.

My mother shook holy water on us as we left and prayed that we come safe home.

We journeyed west through the village. There was smoke coming out of every chimney. Women in red petticoats and white báinín tightly buttoned, with little shawls around their heads were already on their way to milk the cows. They carried mangolds and hay in baskets. The hay would warm up the cattle after the wild night. The animals were protected from the force of the gale by high walls built around sheltered glens among the rocks. When the men were not gathering seaweed, fishing or looking for wrack, they looked after the cattle in bad weather.

Children were up early watching the men going towards the cliffs or enjoying the sight of the waves rearing towards the shore and then dashing themselves against the rocks. They looked enviously at me as I walked proudly along with the wrack hunters, a small coil of rope on my shoulder.

It was half ebb when we got to the Port of the Fort's Mouth. Old villagers who were too shaky to risk the tall cliffs prowled among the boulders picking up a plank here and there. Out in the mouth of the little bay planks were carried back and forth by the current. Now and then a barrel rolled over. What was in the barrels? Rum, oil, grease, tar? We would know later.

My father could hardly restrain the men from picking up stray pieces of timber. " Wait until we get to the Blind Sound," he said. " We'll gather more in one hour there than we would gather here all day."

We walked along the cliff peering at the sea. The surface of the water was unbroken as the wind had died down. Long, lazy swells rolled in from the deep, crested, and broke on the shallows. Every once in a while an exclamation would burst from one of the men :

" Look south-westerly from you, where the sea-gulls are! There's a whole ship load of timber there."

Suddenly I wondered what happened to the sailors who manned the wrecked vessel and I shuddered as I visualised myself going down to death in that terrible sea. Groups of men from Gort na gCapall and from Kilmurvey had picked choice spots along the cliff at and near the Blind Sound. Our advance agents had a good place. The limestone rock on the cliff's edge was smooth and would not fray the cable. The cliff was straight until within five fathoms of the bottom. There were no jutting rocks on the face of the cliff to catch the planks as they were being hauled up.

Nobody had gone down yet as there was very little of the shore at the bottom dry. Planks were piled among the rocks. Sometimes a sea would drive a plank end on against a rock and split it. Men often had their legs broken in similar situations. We were all watching the precious timber below. Hundreds of planks were suddenly left dry by a receding wave.

"Time to go down," said Bartley Pat. The cable

was lashed around his body. He stood on the top of the cliff and took off his cap.

"Now, in the name of the Father, Son and Holy Ghost," he said. He turned his back to the sea, his face to the land and disappeared over the edge.

Little Jimmy was watching the descent from a vantage point and giving us directions with his hands. We lowered gradually. When Bartley had touched bottom we hauled up the rope and let the other two men down. All along the cliff men were descending, dancing in and out, steering themselves with one hand, the other holding on to the rope, striking the cliff with the sole of one foot swinging gracefully out and in until they landed at the bottom. It was a feat that called for daring and experience.

Soon we were hauling up planks and hiding them in the scalps. The coastguards would lay claim to the wrack in the name of the King of England if they found it.

Furiously we worked. The men at the bottom kept sending up planks until the tide came in again. Two of them were hauled up. Then it was Bartley Pat's turn. Little Jimmy raised his hand.

We started to haul. Nobody was watching Jimmy. We were thinking about the timber.

Little Jimmy was frantically signalling us to lower. We payed out the rope slowly. "Very slowly," he signalled. We did not know what was the matter until we brought Bartley to the top.

"I thought I was as dead as a pickled herring," he chuckled. "Little Jimmy thought I gave him the signal to haul while I only wanted more rope. I only had one leg in the coil when ye hauled and I was hoisted half way up the cliff by the ankle."

"You weren't born to be hanged by the legs," my father remarked.

We put in the best part of a week gathering wrack. After the timber was safely stored away in deep clefts and caves, the coastguards visited the village and asked if any timber was washed ashore at the Point of the Fort's Mouth. The villagers advised them that there wasn't a stick to be seen there. The coastguards thanked them for the information and returned to their quarters in Kilronan.

THE LITTLE WAVE

I DOUBT if there is a tougher spot in all Ireland to land your curach in than the Port of the Fort's Mouth, on the south side of Aran between Gort na gCapall and Dún Aonghus. It is the only part of the island on the Atlantic side where the cliffs have been eaten away by the action of the waves, leaving a high *Doorlinn*—a rampart of boulders—to keep back the waves that forever threaten to cut the island in two.

From this little port the fishermen-peasants of Gort na gCapall go out in their canvas-covered curachs to fish bream, pollock, gurnet, ling, eel, and other fish. Twenty years ago and more recently spillet fishing was carried on out of this rocky little port, in the winter time when the wind was to the North and the sea was calm.

When the wind blows in from the Atlantic the mountainous seas make it impossible for even the most courageous fisherman to leave the port. Little spillet fishing is done now. The foreign trawlers are blamed for the scarcity of ling, conger eel, cod, hake and other fish, which the islanders used to catch in great numbers.

One morning about twenty-five years ago, my two cousins and I went out to set spillets from the Port of the Fort's Mouth. It was the morning of St. Brigid's day and the weather was beautiful. The sea was as smooth as a sheltered pond and the water so clear that you could see through it, fathoms deep. The mountains of Kerry were visible, which showed that the atmosphere was clear. It was the loveliest morning I ever bent my back to an oar. We went far out where the white sand is. There's where the large white-bellied conger eels are to be found. We took our markings and set our spillets. More experienced fishermen might have distrusted that calm on a February day.

First we dropped a stone anchor and put a pocán or buoy on the rope. Then we let out the spillets, the hooks of which were baited with mackerel. We stretched them along the ground for a long distance. We put another pocán at the end of the line and rowed into the Port of the Fort's Mouth.

We carried the curach on our backs and laid her down on the limestone flag above high water mark and went on home. During the day my father chanced around the port and discovered that the sea had swollen during the day. In fact but for his fortunate arrival our oars would have been carried away by the waves. He called for help and moved the curach out of danger.

The three of us—my two cousins and I—gathered at the port and discussed whether we should risk going out to take the spillets. If we left them out, there was no knowing what might happen to them, as it might be months before the sea calmed down sufficiently to take them. Yet we would be risking our lives, going out in face of a heavy sea. However, there was no wind.

My father said that if he were in our shoes, he would go out, and my uncle agreed. Both said that if their sons did not have the courage to go out they would go themselves. They uttered lusty oaths and called on all and sundry to witness that if we did not risk our lives taking the spillets the degeneracy of the younger generation would be conclusively proven. We decided to take the chance.

" At half tide you can leave the Little Rough Rock," my father said. " I will watch the Little Wave, and will be able to tell you when there is a long enough lull between the waves to enable you to leave with safety. My brother will help you put the curach on the water."

We got out safely, but when we were on the water, it was rather disconcerting to find ourselves in big troughs of sea and to see the spray dashing as high as fifty feet against the tall cliffs. We rowed out, and finally caught sight of the pocán.

As we hauled in the spillets we could see our mothers watching us from the cliffs, their bright red shawls and red petticoats making them stand out conspicuously against the gray limestone rocks. More often than not we were invisible to them as the curach would sink down between two mighty waves to appear for a moment on the crest of another.

There was little fish—a few skates, ray and an odd conger eel. Fish is very sensitive to a change of weather. The line sometimes got caught on the rocks at the bottom and when this happened we cut it and put a buoy on it. Then we started at the other end. When we got caught we did the same thing again and returned. In the meantime this line would be freed as a rule. Finally we got the lines all in and started for home.

By now it seemed as if the seas were ready to

sweep the whole island away. The waves beat against the cliffs with deafening roars and white pillars of foam rose and fell majestically.

As we neared the shore we could see that all the men and women in the village were awaiting our return. Most of the women were crying. They were all on their knees praying for us. As we rowed into the Port of the Fort's Mouth we could hear my father and my uncle swearing vigorously and pointing to the Little Wave. My father was saying that we could make a landing by running the curach ashore with everything aboard, as there were enough men to meet us in the surf and carry us out of danger. My uncle was swearing that the three men never lived who could bring a curach ashore in such a sea. He suggested that we row around the worst end of the island and land in Port Murvey on the bay side, a distance of fifteen miles. My father beckoned to us to row into a sheltered spot so that he could talk to us.

" Turn her head towards the open sea," he ordered, " and wait beyond the Threshold until I give you the signal. I'll watch for the breakers on the Little Wave, and when there is a *deibhil*, a lull, you'll run her ashore."

We could hear the women crying and praying as wave after wave dashed madly against the jagged rocks. It looked as if the lull would never come. Then suddenly my father took off his black hat and waved to us to row for shore.

" Pull," he shouted ; " pull as you never pulled before. Strengthen the right. Lie on her now. That's it. *Nar laga Dia sibh*—May God not weaken ye ! Straight in as you're going."

With gritted teeth we rowed as we could see a giant breaker rising on the Little Wave. We must be in before the monster catches us. The wave seemed to travel like lightning. Our oars bent under the strain and our breath came in gasps. We were doing my father's bidding.

Suddenly we were seized on both sides by a dozen sturdy fishermen out to their waists in the angry waters. We shipped our oars and rested. We were out of danger. The men staggered and slid on the slippery rocks as they carried us beyond the reach of the waves.

"Twould be a sore calamity to lose any part of that line," said my father, "twill serve a good while yet."

A SOFT, calm, beautiful night in May. I was outside the house leaning on the double wall of the little garden which my father and I had fashioned out of the limestone rocks that once formed the yard of our home. A nice little garden it was. We had blasted the rocks and filled the deep clefts with the fragments. Then we had gone around the crag with baskets and spades and shovels and gathered clay and carried it on our backs to the place we had levelled out. We were careful to build a wall around the cleared space for fear the storms would blow away the loam we put on it. Seaweed and sand we brought from the shore of Kilmurvey, and we scraped the dirt off the low places in the roads where the water had washed it, and in time we had a pretty garden. Now there was cabbage in it and potatoes and other vegetables.

" Time was when the landlord would raise the rent on a man for improving his land," I said to my sister Nora, who was leaning over the wall beside me.

She did not reply. I looked at her and found she was weeping softly. I wanted to tell her to stop, but the words halted in my throat. I was leaving on the morrow for America.

Sounds of revelry came from the kitchen. Martin Dick's melodeon was giving out " The Road to the Wedding," " Miss MacLeod's Reel," and " The Connachtman's Rambles." We could hear the clatter of hob-nailed boots on the earthen floor and the shuffling of pampooties. Shouts of encouragement came from the onlookers, and cries of challenge from the dancers who looked upon this form of amusement as a test of staying power.

The sad murmur of the calm sea at the Port of the Fort's Mouth fell on my ears. This sound had been with me from childhood, and was part of my subconscious being. Everything around me was part of me and I was part of my surroundings. I came out of the rocks and the small patches of soil and out of the sea that surrounded the islands almost as much as I came out of my parents. But this little garden here, came out of me and I felt that it was nearer to me than any other part of the island.

I told Nora to go into the house and enjoy herself

as I wanted to be alone for a little while. When she was gone I made my way over to the Port of the Fort's Mouth to have one last lonely look at those scenes of my childhood.

I lay down on a large flat stone which was raised above the others and looked out over the Little Wave on the limitless waters that touched strange lands. The moon bathed the sea in soft light. I put my elbows on the flag, my hands against my cheeks and put my fingers in my ears. I often did that when near the sea. I heard strange noises as of multitudes speaking in hushed voices. It was the voice of the many-tongued sea, moaning plaintively in my ears.

I walked down to the water's edge and along the beach to the Big Cleft. I picked up a piece of drift wood. What forest did this come out of? What ship did it form part of? Where was this ship wrecked? Well, this little bit of wood was about to end its career as tinder. It would find its way to the hearth of some house in Gort na gCapall, and burn into ashes. It would be thrown out on the dungheap, and in the spring would be spread on a garden as fertilizer. It would be sucked up by a potato stalk and its sap would go into a potato, and this little piece of timber would not be lost, and would never die, but would go on and on until the end of time—if there was any end of time. It was immortal!

I shrugged my shoulders and turned towards home. I would visit the home of Barbara ONeill who was going to America with me.

I had visited Seáinín O Neill's house almost every night during the early spring until it was understood that Barbara and I were to be married in America or else that we would work there for a while, then come home, get married, and settle down in my father's place.

To-night there was no farewell party in Barbara's house, because for one thing there was only one melodeon available and there was more room for dancing in our house. In addition my father and mother were noted throughout the island for their gifts of dancing and singing, my father being the best dancer in the island and my mother the best singer. I learned to dance, but I could not make musical sounds for I had a coarse voice like my father and so had all my sisters but one, who took after my mother.

I dropped into Seáinín O Neill's and found

Barbara and her mother sitting by the fire. The father and the younger children were in bed. The boys and girls who were old enough to go to parties, were at the farewell in our house.

Barbara looked very like her mother, so much so that I almost made an unforgivable mistake one night in the boreen near the well behind their house. I was prowling around hoping Barbara would go to the well for a can of water when I saw a woman dressed just like her, coming out of the house with a tin can. I knelt near the stile over which she would come on her way to the well and as she put her foot on the stone step I stood up. She screamed and when I realised it was Barbara's mother I almost fainted.

" You frightened me," I gasped. " I was just tying the thong of my pampootie."

I did not wait to give further excuses and I was almost certain she knew I was lying, but she was a wise woman and probably in her younger days knew that Seáinín was in danger of making a similar mistake. I never heard a word about the incident afterwards, which raised her in my estimation. I always liked people who were not loose-tongued.

The poor woman was weeping softly, and Barbara was crying. I uttered a loud cheery " May God bless all here! " and I was answered with, " May God and the Glorious Virgin bless you."

" What is all this crying about? " I asked.

At this Barbara wept out loud and her mother wiped her eyes in her check apron. Barbara adjourned to her room where I could hear the bed creak as she threw herself on it and sobbed. This going to America was the nearest thing to death. It was a life sentence of exile, except in rare cases. Poverty drove them away and poverty would keep them away, for the most of them were doomed to slave for a master and remain on the brink of want for the rest of their lives.

" Musha, Taimín," the poor woman said, " it seems that it is only yesterday she was running around my knees and now she is going and I am afraid I'll never see her again. May God and the Glorious, Charitable Virgin forgive me for crying over the will of the good God Almighty."

" The good God Almighty has no more to do with it than one of those hens roosting on that pole," I said, pointing to the hens perched on a pole that stretched along the top of the wall of the kitchen from the edge of the loft over the large sleeping room to the other loft over the small sleeping rooms. " There is nothing for her here and even if you only had herself and you could give her the place maybe it would be better for her to go."

" Sure I don't know," she whimpered. " Some say everything is God's will.

I did not reply. Suddenly it came to me that it might be a good thought to go into the room and comfort Barbara.

" She is very lonesome," I said, pointing to the room.

" Her heart is breaking, Taimín. I wish you'd look after her out there."

" I will do that," I said.

I walked into the room. It was dark but for the moonlight that came through the small window. Barbara was lying face down on the bed. I went over to her and shook her.

" Get up and stop your crying! " said I.

She went on sobbing. I put my hand on her head, then on her face. She did not stir. Then I put my hands under her waist and tried to lift her. She would not be lifted. I threw myself on the bed alongside of her and put one arm around her. With my other hand I turned over her face to me and kissed her lips. She kissed me in return. I was almost delirious with joy. Sweet tremors danced through my blood. I put my arms around her and pulled her towards me. She threw her arms around me and we were silent for a while.

" We'll get married in America," I whispered.

" We will, Taimín! " she said.

We walked into the kitchen. Barbara's eyes were dry. Her face was radiant. I had my hand on her shoulder. Her mother glanced up at us. Then she arose and throwing her arms around her daughter she kissed her fervently and cried softly. Then she embraced me and called me her " little son."

When I appeared at the farewell party later the people asked me where I was, but I did not enlighten them.

" Taking a last look around," I said carelessly.

Somebody said that my father and I should dance a hornpipe together.

" Give us ' The Flowers of Edinboro,' Martin,"
my father said to Martin Dick. This was what
my father called a double reel, and he liked it
for hornpipes.

We danced the first step together. Then we
danced every second one until we danced twenty-
four separate steps. There wasn't a word spoken
while we were on the floor. I don't think either
one of us ever danced better. When we finished
there wasn't a dry eye in the house. My father
walked outside. There was a faint streak of dawn
coming from behind the Cliff of the Little Fort to
the North-East. A little later when I walked out I
saw him leaning against the wall looking towards
the east. I did not intrude on his moment of
abandoned grief.

Songs were sung. There was more dancing.
Poitín was drunk and those who would drink no
liquor, drank tea. Young boys and girls flirted in
the shadows. For my father and mother and me
and my sisters it was a night of sorrow. My mood
was more attuned to the lonesome murmur of
the sea than to the lifting lilt of the melodeon.

My father sang a song—a fighting song—in his
harsh voice. Like many of the fighting songs of

the Irish it was a sad song. The songs of a country accustomed to defeat are sad.

> Where bullets loud rattle and cannon comes rolling by
> Oh, it was in that battle sweet Drathaireen Oh, mo
> Chroidhe (Sweet brother of my heart) did die.

"Musha *nár laga Dia thú!*—may God not weaken you!" said a neighbour. "It's you that has the heart."

"*Gaibhtear fonn le fonn agus fonn le mio-fhonn,*" my father said. "Songs are sung with joy and songs are sung in sorrow."

My mother must sing. The people insisted. They ought to know how hard it would be on her but they insisted. She complied at last. Her voice was sweet, very sweet and plaintive.

> The glorious sun descending dies,
> With crimson rays the western skies
> The wild winds come with mournful sighs
> Across the silent sea.
>
> .   .   .   .   .   .
>
> Ah, once this hour was dear to me
> But now it has come and I deplore
> For I'll see my love no more.

Morning followed dawn. Most of the merry-makers left for their homes. I laid down to have a few winks of sleep. I would be leaving on the *Dúras* in the afternoon.

Father David O Maille was over early.

" Let us walk a while! " he suggested.

We walked towards the highway, without speaking, a good part of the way.

" You will not forget Ireland," he said.

" Never," I answered.

We were silent again.

" There's something I have to ask you, Father O Maille," I said.

" What is it Tom? "

" Why is it that fathers and mothers in Ireland raise children in pain and toil, only to see them driven off to foreign lands by the spectre of poverty? "

" It's the will of God," he said calmly.

I made no comment.

" We are going to have fine weather," I remarked, looking out at the sea in the bay.

At the head of the road we stopped. We looked westward at the fine, green fertile fields on the land-grabber's estate, the only worth-while land on the island. The landgrabber was dead, but the estate belonged to his family still.

" I would like you to kneel, Tomás, and let me give you my blessing," the priest said, with a soft look in his eyes.

I knelt down on the road.

When I arose he gave me a medal, shook hands with me, and turning the bend of the road, walked towards his home without saying a word.

My mother bid me her last private farewell in the room where she often smoothed my hair and dried my tears and made me laugh with her funny stories. My heart seemed to swell until only torrents of tears could relieve the strain on my chest.

" Don't forget God, Tomás," she said.

The women of the village were in and they all crying. Crying for my mother they were. It would be their turn some other time. The men talked about fishing.

Little Jimmy shook my hand and turned away. Colm of the Shaggy Beard, gruff as ever, hoped I'd have a lot of fun with the women. Patsy Holland said nothing, but looked over my head out of his melancholy, wise eyes.

My dog Oscar followed me. He knew there was something wrong. He sneaked along by the side of the road. When I stopped and looked at him, he sidled up to me. I fondled him and there were tears in my eyes. He whined and licked my face.

" I'll never see you again, Oscar! " I said.

I hated to drive him home. He retreated slowly, stopping to look back every now and then. Then he stopped, sat on his haunches and howled.

*   *   *

The whistles of the *Dúras* blew three times. I had said good-bye to my mother, my sisters, and all those nearest to me, many times. My father was standing apart with his two hands in his vest pocket. How well he could cover up his grief!

I stepped aboard the *Dúras*. My father followed. He beckoned me to come behind the cabin where we could not be seen. Then he threw his arms around me and his tears fell on my face. It was the first time I ever knew him to weep or make any show of affection.

" If you ever want to come back, son, the place is yours," he said.

Then he walked off the boat and up the pier. As the boat pulled out I could see him walking steadily along the road that skirted the bay. He never looked back.

My mother stayed on the edge of the pier until she was only a blur in the distance.

Barbara ONeill was leaning over the side of the vessel, her tears dropping into the water. I stood by her side and put my hand on her shoulder. But no words came to my tongue.

I looked steadily into the swirling water. My eye caught a bubble as it arose. For one brief moment it rested on the surface of the rushing sea. Then it sank.

The *Dúras* sped on, making for Galway and the great world beyond.

THE NEXT DAY we were to land in Galway. The great liner was thrashing her way through heavy seas and the severest storm she had met since leaving New York. Giant waves struck her with the force of ten thousand trip hammers, making her shudder from stem to stern. Deck seats were torn adrift and thrown here and there. Nobody slept. A rumour went the rounds that the captain would not bring the vessel to Galway with such a gale raging in from the west.

All night the big seas kept pounding away. Towards morning it calmed down considerably. Those of us who were to land in Galway were up before the dawn. The rumour of the night before was unfounded. The liner was making direct for the old City of the Tribes. She would pass to the south of the Aran Islands and of my native village Gort na gCapall which I had left twenty-one years ago and never visited since.

With the first streak of dawn a light glimmered in the distance. It was from the lighthouse on the

most westerly of the two little rocky that lie outside Aran Mór. My grandfather on the mother's
side, one Thomas Ganly, built it some eighty years
ago.

My mother often told me interesting stories
about him. He visited many countries building
lighthouses and piers. His father was an Orangeman, who married a Catholic girl, and my grandfather and a sister of his followed the Catholic faith.
My grandfather was as intolerant in religious
matters as his father had been tolerant. It was
often my mother told me of his fights for the faith
in Orange strongholds. In one of those fights he
had his skull cracked by a blow of a chair, wielded
by an infuriated Orangeman who did not like my
grandfather's attitude towards the glorious, pious
and immortal William! How the Orangeman
fared in the fight I never heard.

He came to Aran building lighthouses and
piers. There he met my grandmother who was
the descendant of a colourful character who went
by the name of *Mícheál Riabhach* (Speckled
Michael). Mícheál was a successful smuggler,
and had picked out a nice grassy plot for himself
in the village of Mainistir there to end his days

when he got weary of smuggling. My grand-father liked Mainistir and decided to drop anchor there.

But he had not much interest in farming, and what little he had never resulted in profit. He could not tell his own sheep from a neighbour's and one day as he was passing by one of his fields he saw a number of sheep in it which he mistook for those of a villager for whose honesty he had little regard.

" Bad luck to that thieving Pat Mór," he muttered, as he knocked down the gap and drove the sheep to the pound. Returning home he threatened to flog his son for not keeping an eye on his land. My grandmother wept and said he would send her to the poorhouse. He had to pay twopence each to get his own sheep out of the pound.

The lighthouse is there as solid as ever but the engineer who built it is dust. " Many a thing is more lasting than a person," the Aran islanders say.

I felt anything but cheerful approaching my island home, or what was once my home. My parents and many of my boyhood friends were in the graveyards of the island. Most of my other associates had gone to America to " make their fortunes." The sight of the lighthouse and the thoughts of my blood relationship with it had a galvanizing effect on me. After all I was closer to the things that mattered in this barren island than I was in the materially richer country whence I came. The liner sped on and now we could see the outline of Aran Mór like a flat green cloud on the horizon. I stood as if glued to the rail, recollections chasing each other through my mind.

Brannock Island can be seen now. Then across a narrow channel the village of Bungowla with its little bay protected from the Atlantic swells by the Black Rock of Woe which takes the strength out of the waves that dash unceasingly against its jagged crest.

At Bungowla the island slopes down to the sea on every side. A fairly prosperous fishing village when there was a good demand for mackerel. Kelpmaking was also a source of wealth. Small fields could be seen here and there among the rocks. Almost every rood of cultivated land in Bungowla was made by the people. My one recollection of Bungowla is that I used to lie on the rocks with a friend when I was a boy to shoot at cormorants as they flew southwards to their homes in the tall cliffs. They flew low and close to the land at this point.

On goes the liner and we are now opposite Creig a Chéirín. The land rises sharply from Bungowla and from the shore on the Conamara side of the island and steeply to a height of two hundred and fifty feet on the south. The land here is even poorer than in Bungowla, though it seems impossible. The cow droppings are used as a substitute for peat, and but for the constant fertilizing of the land with seaweed it would in time produce neither grass nor vegetables. The island is peatless and almost treeless, and when the peasant fishermen have not enough money to buy turf from the Conamara men or when the weather is so bad that the turf boats cannot come in they are obliged to burn dry dung as fuel. In fact dry cow dung makes a bright clean fire, and the more thrifty of the islanders never allow a bit of it to go to waste. Experts in cow dung fuel could tell you what kind of cattle feed produces the best substitute for turf.

In the tall cliff to the south of Creig a Chéirín is

the Piper's Castle and the secret underground path that runs from the Atlantic to the Red Lake on the bay side of the island. Here an outlaw piper from Conamara hid from the minions of the law, and never appeared to the eye of man again. The natives did not inquire into the nature of his crime. It was enough for them to know that he was hunted by the British Government. Food and shelter they gave him, and then he vanished. Legend has it that he still plays mournful tunes on his pipes, but nobody wants to hear the music for it is believed that the person hearing it will before long be called to the Piper's Castle from which there is no returning.

In those cliffs, wild birds nest on the ledges that run for miles along the face of them. Indentations are made in the gravel seams between the layers of rock by wind and water. Here guillemot and cormorant, seagull and *crosán* (puffin) lay their eggs and hatch out their young.

In my youth, expert cliffmen had themselves lowered down in the evening to those ledges and they lay around them all night killing birds and gathering eggs in the season. In the morning they would have the birds hauled up to the top of the cliff. Sometimes they scaled the cliffs alone and unaided. The most famous of the cliffmen is now too old to climb, but he cannot resist the temptation to stand on the verge of a narrow slab of stone that juts out from the top of the cliff at Creig a Chéirín and look down.

Every rock and cranny along those cliffs has an appropriate name and I recollected the thrill I got from looking for pieces of wreckage among the giant boulders at the foot of those cliffs when I was a boy. And when I found a barrel, or a piece of board with the name of a foreign country on it I and other boys of the village used to wonder what this strange country was like or if its people were like ourselves.

We pass Creig a Chéirín. The cliffs grow taller. We are opposite Eoghanacht, the site of one of the four forts in Aran Mór. Archaeologists are in doubt about the origin of those fortresses, when they were built or by whom. But I came to the conclusion that the builders had a keen appreciation of the value of land, for this and the other forts in the island command the choicest pieces of land in Aran Mór. From the tall cliffs on the south of Eoghanacht to the sloping beach on the north there is a fairly decent pasturage, water is abundant, there are some large fields on which the soil is from four to six inches deep while the shore on the Conamara side is one of the best in the island for seaweed.

This stretch of land once belonged to the peasantry of Eoghanacht, but a namesake of mine took a fancy to it and gave the tenants the choice of accepting their transportation to America or being thrown out on the road without any compensation. Some of them went to America and others stayed at home. Many things have happened in Ireland since then, but the descendants of those tenants are still landless. The landgrabber's heirs lost Eoghanacht as well as another section that was acquired in a somewhat like manner. My father who was the chief leader of the Land League movement in Aran was one of those responsible for the landgrabber's tribulations, yet it came to pass that a sister of mine married the man who purchased this estate. . .

I am now looking at the level field with the short sweet grass on top of the cliff where she and I often stood of a fine day looking out at the Brandon mountains ; I telling her that some day

I would be going out that way to foreign countries,
Australia maybe, perhaps the United States,
or even to the Argentine, and she listening and
hoping I would stay at home and amuse her with
my fanciful stories, settle down in the old home-
stead and get married, die in my dotage and be
buried with my ancestors.

People would say that nobody could have luck
with land that was grabbed from the peasantry.
People " say more than their prayers," for if this
were so the " best people " in Ireland would not
have any luck for they have inherited their broad
acres from plunderers. My brother-in-law paid
for this farm with money he earned in the United
States, and there was no odium attached to his
acquisition of it. My sister never saw me off to
the United States. She died long before I fled the
parental nest. My brother-in-law died. The *Teach
Mór* (Big House) he built is untenanted.

I am glad when I see the noble fort of Dún
Aonghus, cresting the tallest cliff in the island,
three hundred feet from sea level. It awakens
more pleasant memories.

The fort comprises three rings of horseshoe-
shaped walls overlooking Port Murvey and the

best land in Aran. This is where the landgrabber's cattle were walked blind-folded over the cliff during the stirring days of the Land League. But for the Land League the whole island might have been his by grace of the landlord. Near Port Murvey on the bay side is the village of Kill-murvey. The villagers were allowed to live on the land the grabber thought not worth taking. For generations they have been hauling sand from the seashore, mixing it with seaweed and silt from the roads and turning bare rocks into tillage land. Someone has written that "angels from heaven must have poured down blessings on the bare flags of Aran" otherwise the land could not produce the finest cattle and sheep in Ireland, and excellent crops of potatoes.

It is quite possible that the angels took a friendly interest in the island, if for no other reason than because of the number of saints who settled there and built monasteries, but it must be admitted that the angels were ably assisted by the hard-working peasants who broke rocks with sledges, levelled out the area about to be "made," carried precious soil in creels on their backs and often-times fought fierce battles with rivals to gain possession of the loam to mix with the loose sand and yellow clay. The Gaedhealtacht peasant is oftentimes charged with laziness by superior persons from other parts of Ireland who themselves failed to make a living out of good tillage and pasture land, but if any one of these critics had to rear a family of from ten to fourteen children on sixteen or twenty-four acres of Aran Mór or the other two islands in the chain he would have a different story.

We pass Dún Aonghus. The landscape now becomes even more familiar. There is the Cliff of the Swan and the Blind Sound, where the steep descent of the land from Dún Aonghus stops. Underneath the cliff at this spot the sea has bored a deep hole. For centuries the ocean has waged a winning battle against the rock. It aims to cut the island in two. Time is on its side and the sea is patient. I see the Yellow Rock where I caught my first bollach and the Worm Hole, that remarkable oblong hole, like a Roman bath, carved out of the limestone flag. It ebbs and flows through an underground passage. There should be a legend about the Worm Hole, but if there is I never heard it. It is about time one should be invented.

Now we are opposite the Port of the Fort's Mouth and the village of Gort na gCapall. An ancestor of mine by the name of Bartholomew founded Gort na gCapall. I am sorry he did not pick a choicer location.

There is a story they tell in Aran about a wealthy Englishman who suddenly became aware of his conscience and wanted to go to some remote and desolate spot to live the simple life and do penance for his sins. He travelled the world and selected Gort na gCapall, as being in his opinion the most desolate place on the map. He offered the villagers a large sum of money for the townland, but they laughed his offer to scorn and went on braving the wild seas off the Port of the Fort's Mouth in their curachs searching for fish, carrying seaweed on their backs up steep cliffs, making land out of rock, filling fissures in the crags with stones for fear the cattle might break their legs in them, making kelp, fighting landlords and tax gatherers and living rather happily in the place a wealthy Englishman had selected for his Purgatory.

Bartholomew's descendants still live in Gort na gCapall, and work with the primitive implements Bartholomew and the men of his time used.

Bartholomew built his house upon a rock, not for reasons of security or because he considered the rock symbolical of continuity, but because he did not want to waste a piece of good pasture or tillage land under a house.

Directly opposite Gort na gCapall is the village of Oatquarter, where in the old schoolhouse, now a ruin, David O Callaghan taught me to read and write my native language thirty odd years ago.

My most treasured recollection of Oatquarter national school is the memory of Roger Casement, tall and thin, his black beard accentuating the pallor of his countenance. I believe he was British Consul at Lisbon at the time. He visited the school house and told the teacher he would like to know if he had a pupil who could grind his way through Eoghan Ó Neachtain's column in the *Cork Examiner*. The teacher fondled his luxuriant brown beard and smiled. " Indeed I have," he said. I was called to the front and came out of the test with drums beating. Sir Roger gave me half-a-crown, and afterwards sent me three books: *The Story of Ireland*, by A. M. Sullivan; *Séadna*, by Father O Leary; and *Fairies at Work*, by William P. Ryan, then the editor of the *Irish*

Peasant. The two latter books were in Gaelic. Later Sir Roger planned to send me to Summerhill College, Sligo, but fate intervened and the project fell through.

Mr. O Callaghan had no word of Irish when he came to Aran. He learned the old tongue and after he had mastered it he impressed upon the islanders the importance of preserving it and taught them to pride themselves on its possession. In those days the islands were being rapidly Anglicised. Policemen, tax collectors, and the native shopkeeping shoneens were at work hammering a sense of inferiority into the people. " English is the language that'll stand by you when you go to America," was the maxim. Children were reared for export to the American labour market.

Mr. O Callaghan did great work. He was no cheap Jingo nationalist of the type who froths at the mouth at the mention of an Englishman; but he hated British imperialism with all its works and pomps. He was the first *Sinn Féiner* in the island, and had no difficulty in making one of me. My father threw in his lot with us, when he learned that there were not more than four hundred

Sinn Féiners in all Ireland. He was a strong be-
liever in minorities and was always ready to side
with the underdog.

As the liner sneaked along in the now
smooth sea I wondered where my old school-
teacher was, if he were still alive, and if he
recollected the many tricks I played on him for
which he thrashed me with violence and with
demoniacal fury. He was a fine man. How many
workers like O Callaghan are forgotten when the
ideals for which they struggled are realized in
whole or in part, while the blatant politicians
and the gentlemen who always manage to pick
the winning side are honoured?

The cliffs are rising steadily again since we left
the Port of the Fort's Mouth, the only beach on
the south side of the island. The next village is
Comhrac, which means conflict. The English
post-office name for the hamlet is meaningless,
like the phonetic atrocities that go for names of
places all over Ireland. Comhrac is distinguished
for having the best seaweed shore in Aran Mór,
and for being the site of the church of the Four
Beautiful Saints, set in a sheltered plot where the
grass grows long and green all the year round.

Next comes the village of Baile na Creige which is, as the name implies, unusually rocky. Here lives the famous cliffman, cobbler, dog-fancier, and amateur archaeologist, Michaleen son of Sarah. He claims to have discovered diamonds in the boulders by the seashore. Baile na Creige, like all the other villages in Aran Mór, cannot be seen from the south. The island rises in tiers from the bay and most of the hamlets are sheltered by low cliffs from the storms that come from the west.

The next townland is Eochaill, the site of one of the two Catholic churches in the island, a fort and an old disused lighthouse. The chapel is on the sloping lawn over the road overlooking the bay. Here I served Mass when a boy, and when I had outgrown the soutane my brother Liam took my place and my soutane!

How I used to envy the men and the young boys of my own age who lay on the grass outside the church before Mass, talking and laughing while I and my associate altar-boy stood in the sacristy waiting for the arrival of the priest. And how great used to be my satisfaction in ringing the bell and seeing the idlers on the lawn jump to their feet and make a rush for a seat in the gallery.

And when the people were all gathered in church I carried the pail of holy water for the priest and the sprinkler made out of straw, and sometimes when a large face with all the earmarks of piety got an extra splash of holy water, I chuckled inwardly and glanced at the priest's face to see if his generosity was intentional.

I remember one curate who doubted the sincerity of those who ostentatiously manifested their piety by loud groans and moans during Mass, and he often expressed himself frankly on this subject in his sermons. . . . .

The steamer is streaking her way rapidly over the smooth sea, but she is not moving more rapidly than my thoughts. One moment I am in Aran, the next in Boston, New York, Chicago, Montana, London, Paris, Berlin, Moscow. From Aran with its primitive economy to America, the last word in industrial efficiency. From Aran where nobody got rich or even wished for riches, to America where some made fabulous fortunes and almost everybody hoped his turn would come! Leaving Aran when the world was peaceful and full of hope, with only a black speck here and there on the political horizon to keep the pessimists in good mood. Returning when the world is black with despair, the bubble of prosperity burst, wars and civil strife the order of the day, and world war rumours in the air!

Leaving Aran twenty-one years ago with the Union Jack flying over police barrack and coast-guard station. Returning to see the tricolour of a Free State of twenty-six of our thirty-two counties flying in its place—a tricolour designed to be the flag of an All-Ireland Republic. Inter-vening years of civil war and bloodshed. Millions of human lives sacrificed to human greed. The noble Casement whose great heart went out to all suffering humanity, to the slaves of the notorious King Leopold of Belgium in the Congo, and the unfortunate chattels of the rubber exploiters in the Putumayo, South America, as well as to the Irish people who chafed under British rule—Casement dies on the gallows, killed by the Government that knighted him for his humanitarian work in the Congo. Did the British capitalists covet King Leopold s rubber? Did they hanker for his slave-gotten loot? Connolly, Pearse . . . The liner speeds on.

We are now opposite the little village of

Mainistir, snuggling unseen by me under the hills overlooking a small bay. The village that was more home to me than my native Gort na gCapall. It was my mother's birthplace. And I liked the emotional, soft, witty, story-telling Ganlys better than the harsh, quarrelsome, haughty, " ferocious O Flaherties." Only one Ganly left in Aran : a cousin of mine. She married an O Flaherty. All my Ganly aunts and uncles dead. Father William died in Melbourne. A fine Gaelic scholar, melancholy and joyous in turns. My uncle Thomas who took a shot at a bailiff during the Land League days and went to America, after being released from prison, where he was held as a " suspect " with my father—he died in Boston. My uncle Pat, carefree and irresponsible who inherited the family estate—he took the landlord's eviction notices and other essential documents out of the courthouse during the Land League days. A great rebel, the best story-teller in Aran, and my favourite relative. My Aunt Kate who died with a witticism on her lips. Aran would be cold without them! The little green fields of Mainistir, the little ruined temple under the ivy-clad hill, the little well where I used to go with my cousins to get water for the tea, the low cliff outside the door of the house on which my uncle used to stand and tease the men working in the garden—they would revive old memories. Well——

Dún Dubh Chathair, strikes the eye. It's the last of the forts in Aran Mór. We are now in line with Kilronan, the largest village on the island.

Next comes Killeany, a fishing village of land-less peasants forced to depend entirely on the sea for their existence. They were robbed of their land by Aran's greatest landgrabber. When the seas were rough, they could not fish, so they sat on the walls or lay on the limestone flags. Superior persons said they were very poor because they were very lazy. They were very poor because they had been robbed.

Beyond Killeany—called after Aran's greatest saint, Enda—is the graveyard. On the sandy mound over a long strand. Here is where the bones of my people rest.

We pass Iar Arainn, the most easterly village and sand-swept. We sight the lighthouse on Straw Island at the entrance to Kilronan. We pass Gregory's Sound, Inismaan, the Foul Sound, and then Inisheer. Now we are heading for the great Bay of Galway.

I look backwards at the islands that are now flattening themselves out like blue mists on the horizon, and a pang goes through me, as it did twenty-one years before, when they faded from my view. But only for a moment. I'll be back in a few days. The giant steamer sneaks up by the County Clare that slopes sharply to the sea at Ceann Bóirne. We seem to be within a few yards of the land when the mighty chains rumble and we are at anchor. Up comes the tender and we get ready for the shore.

Irish immigration officers (with a queer thrill I see the " Harp without a Crown " on their caps) examine our passports. About three hundred passengers are landing in Galway. For many years this magnificent port was neglected by the Atlantic liners. But the competition of German and American ships forced the British lines to place the western capital of Ireland on their calling lists.

A member of the tender's crew looked familiar.

" You wouldn't be the Thomas Cook who used to be on the old *Duras* by any chance?" I asked. " Or his son?"

" The same Thomas Cook," he said, with a smile and a shake hands. " How are you, Tomás? I heard you were coming home. Your sister and her little daughter will meet you at the dock."

" You look as young as you did the day I left home," I said.

" Life here is easier than in America," he replied.

" I suppose Michael Folan is dead," I asked. " He was mate on the *Duras* when I was a child."

" Faith he isn't. You'll meet him at the dock."

" Does nobody ever die around Galway Bay? "

" They do, bydad, my own father died. God rest him. I'll have to be moving. I'll see you later."

The tender pulled away. Passengers bound for Cobh and Liverpool crowded the rails bidding farewells to those on the tender. Friendships had been formed during the seven-day trip from New York. Few of them would outlive the first day ashore.

An Irishman who ran a dancing academy in New York was making his annual pilgrimage to Ireland. If the depression that had America by the throat continued much longer those visits would be less frequent. The collapse of American prosperity would be felt around the world.

" How is business going to be revived? " I asked the dancing magnate.

" Roosevelt will bring back prosperity," he answered confidently. " The country is fundamentally sound. The depression is purely psychological. The people have got to start spending again. Hoarding should be made a jail offence. Money must be put back in circulation and kept in circulation."

Such a simple solution of the great problem had never occurred to me. I kept thinking about this easy road to prosperity until the tender rounded a headland and the City of Galway spread out before us. I saw a knot of people on a grassy plot and wondered where the dock was located. The tender sidled up to this green headland and proceeded to unload us.

Here at the gangplank was Michael Folan.

" *Céad Fáilte Rómhat*—a hundred welcomes before you. If I didn't know it was you, I wouldn't know you," he said.

" *Go mairidh tú*—May you live! " I replied.

167

"You didn't lose the Irish anyway, and that's more than can be said for some others," he said.

"You look disgustingly young and healthy," I said.

"Too busy to worry about my health," he replied.

"Nevertheless," I said, "in common decency you should try to look your age." He went his way smiling.

GALWAY. Here was Galway, looking to my travelled eyes no larger than a city block in New York. The first time I visited the city the size of it frightened me and I was careful not to get far from our lodgings for fear I might lose my way. I stayed with my mother in a little house near the fish market. Men and women slept in the same room. Accommodation was scarce in those days. The man whose bed I shared was a stone cutter. In the morning he had two raw eggs and a glass of milk for breakfast. His health was delicate, I remember being told.

At night boys and girls gathered on the concrete where the peddlers retailed fish in the morning. The melodeon music sounded sweet and plaintive, and far into the night I could hear the clatter of boots on the cement and merry laughter from the dancers. How I wished to stay in Galway ! Dancing and music in Aran at that period was almost exclusively confined to weddings.

I wandered through the lanes near the lodging-house and peered into doorways. No grass on the streets! How different to the " streets " of my native village! I recollect a buxom redhaired woman sitting on a doorstep with a loaf of bread in her hand. She called me over and insisted that I accept a piece of the loaf from her. I took the bread and ran away in terror. I threw it into an alley when I got out of her sight. When I told my mother about it she said I did wrong, that it was a sin to throw away bread. " Many is the poor person would like to have it," she said.

What stories I heard about Galway when I was a boy! Of the battles between the Aran Islanders and the men of Castlegar. The feud started over the buying of a beast. It was alleged that a Castlegar man defrauded an Aran Islander. Blackthorn sticks were called into play. Two mainlanders by the name of Joyce and two Aranmen named O Flaherty and Connolly were the heroes of the tales told around the turf fires of Gort na gCapall on winter evenings. The Joyces, each wielding two sticks stood back to back and defended themselves for hours against a small army of islanders. In another part of the battlefield O Flaherty and Connolly waded through the foe as Conán Maol did through the hordes of the King of Sorcha in the *Adventures of Lomnachtáin*.

When the islanders came to Galway to a fair, peddlers met them at the docks and did a brisk trade in blackthorn sticks. The islanders in those days were suspicious of *muinntir na tíre*—the people of the country. Their allies were the men from the wilds of Conamara whose ancestors had colonised the islands.

The little fishing village of Cladach, a part of Galway City, had a great fascination for me. Irish was the language of those fishermen, though across the Corrib bridge in the town Gaelic was rarely used by the townspeople. The Cladach people still clung to some of the decentralised democratic usages of the old clan system. They elected their own magistrate and abided by his rulings. He qualified for the honour by being the most intrepid fighter and the most daring fisherman in the community.

In May the Cladach men sailed out to the south of Aran Mór in their little sailing boats fishing for gurnet. There they met the men of Gort na gCapall in curachs. The Cladach men had fires in their boats and they cooked fish which they swapped with the islanders. "*Cnúdán bruighte er dhá chnúdán fuar*—one boiled gurnet for two raw ones," was their trading cry. But when the islanders visited the Cladach in a merry mood and taunted the fishermen with this cry a battle ensued.

And then there was the story of the giant Negro from the West Indies who arrived on a steamer and went around the town to see the sights. He drank more gin than was conducive to a mellow outlook on life in general and on Galway in particular, so he challenged the inhabitants to single combat. The black man hooted his way through the main streets of the city calling on the young men to come out and fight. He returned to his ship with a bloodless victory to his credit.

It was a case of "see Galway and die" with me and the boys of my age. Dublin, London, Paris, New York and other large cities might be large but Galway was colossal. Yet we believed that when Galway ended its career as the capital of Christendom it would be Aran's turn: "*Bl'atha an Rí bhí, Gaillimh atá agus Árainn a bhéas* —Athenry that was, Galway that is and Aran that will be" this was the prophecy.

In the morning the fishwives bought the fish from the Cladach men and went round the streets with skibs on their heads, arms akimbo, selling it. They sang out their wares in various tones of voice. One would shout shrilly : " Aran bream! Aran bream!" Another " Fu-rressh herring! Fu-rressh herring!" or "Fu-rressh gurnet!" or "Fu-rreesh mackerel!" After the fish was sold the women relaxed in publichouses. In the evenings they sang ballads in the streets.

Then there was Tommy Réamoinn's—Thomas MacDonagh—bad-tempered jennet who could carry the entire cargo of the *Duras* if it could be piled on his back. He became a myth in Aran.

Nothing that could be given a humorous twist escaped my mother's observation while she was in Galway. She could puncture the inflated bladder of shoddy respectability and pretence with artistic skill. She would store up enough impressions of Galway and the people she met there during each trip to entertain our visitors for the best part of a year.

The Customs shed was a chaos of baggage. When I located mine I looked round for a Customs officer. I spied a man in blue uniform talking to a girl.

" Are you a Customs officer?" I asked.

" Yes," he said.

" Then would you mind casting the old eagle eye on my baggage?" I asked, in Babbitarian Americanese.

" Sure thing," he said. To the girl : " Excuse me for a moment."

I offered to open my baggage.

" Personal effects?" he asked, chalk poised.

" Yes."

Down came the chalk with unerring precision, leaving marks that signified " O.K."

He resumed his interesting conversation.

It was Thursday—two days before Christmas Eve. The *Dún Aonghus* was schedule to sail for the islands Saturday morning, " weather and other circumstances permitting."

On Friday a storm raged and rain came down in torrents. I had intended to visit familiar spots, but the weather kept me indoors. Early Saturday morning I was on the pier. There was nobody in sight. The boat was getting up steam. I heard the measured tread of a man in hobnailed boots on the paving behind me. I turned round. It was Little Martin, a comrade of my boyhood days. Cheeks with the tan of the sea wind on them, raven black hair, not a speck of gray, eyes that danced in their sockets with health and vitality—that was Little Martin, six feet two inches of him. I saluted him in Gaelic.

" What do you think of the day Little Martin? " I asked, gesturing towards the islands. He answered slowly.

" Well now, I don't want to be considered unmannerly but if you are not Thomas Mike Micheál Phádraig I'll eat the first *banbh* that comes down the quay," he said.

" You're not going to eat any raw young pig to-day, Martin," I answered. The greeting was cordial and lengthy. We talked about personal matters.

" The village won't look the same now without the old people," he said. " You know I'm living in Oatquarter. When I go up to Gort na gCapall I always feel lonely. I'm the only one of the family left in Aran. It will be hard on you, too."

I nodded. He fished in a trawler all around the

Irish coast and was now going home for his first
visit in five years.

" Sure the house might have been carried away
by a hurricane since I was there last," he said,
with a burst of laughter. Then seriously : " Lots
of things have happened since you left. It isn't
the same way at all people look at things now."
Then after a brief hesitation : " It is harder
to fool them now than it was in your time.
Maybe I'm wrong, but that's the way it looks
to me."

People were now streaming towards the boat,
some with baskets filled with groceries, or parcels
in check aprons. Donkey carts filled with bonhams
rumbled along. Trucks were delivering goods
for shipment to the islands. Bags of flour, oatmeal,
and bran were hoisted into the hold ; also barrels
of oil. Yes and herrings from Aberdeen!

" Sounds like the old gag about ' hauling coals
to Newcastle, ' " I said.

" Well, you see, we lost the British market for
fresh mackerel and the American market for
pickled mackerel and herring," he explained.

" But what about the Irish market? " I asked.
" Have the Irish people stopped eating fish? "

" No, but the poor can't afford to eat Irish fish.
It costs too much. British and Scotch fish is
much cheaper."

" Now, that's queer," I said. " I thought the
Department of Fisheries was subsidising the Irish
fishing industry and regulating the price of fish."
He looked at me with considerable amusement
and his eyes danced with merriment.

" Queer? " he chuckled. " Sure it's queer.
There is a subsidy all right, but some people say
it's the fellow who owns the trawler who gets the
subsidy whether his boat catches any fish or not.
Anyhow I bet you couldn't get a bit of fresh fish
in Aran now if you gave your two eyes for it.
Did you know that there is not a single sailing
boat leaving Kilronan now? When we were boys
there were sometimes as many as forty-five in the
mackerel and fishing seasons. Of course the Inismaan people fish the same as ever."

" Then maybe it's the fault of the people of
Aran Mór," I said.

" It is and it isn't. They were geared for
mackerel and herring fishing and went out for
ling, eel and that kind of fish only seldom. The
foreign trawlers are doing that now and the men

of the island can't compete with them in curachs and sailing boats."

" But why don't they catch enough for their own consumption? "

" Arrah, there's nobody there compared to what there used to be. If America kept going as it was for a few more years there wouldn't be a man in the island except the blind, the halt and the lame.

THE WHISTLE blew and we went aboard. The steamer was crowded with islanders from Inisheer, Inismaan, and Aran Mór. The men and women of Inisheer and Aran Mór were dressed partly in homespun and partly in factory-made garments. The dress of the Inismaan people was almost entirely of island manufacture, outside of Cashmere shawls and boots on the women and plaid shirts and boots on the men who did not wear pampooties. The petticoats worn by the girls were a flaming red, contrasting pleasantly with the blue and white in the men's garments.

The *Dún Aonghus* pulls out and soon we are tossing in a rough sea. The weather is cold and Little Martin and I retire to the cabin.

There is an old man with a game leg holding forth to an interested audience.

" I'm for De Valera and I don't care who knows it," he said challengingly. " Whatever else he may do he's done one thing that the people of Aran should thank him for the longest day they'll live. He got them atin' mate. They're atin' their own pork, beef and mutton now instead of the fat American bacon they used to bring from Galway with them to put flavour on the cabbage, after they sold their own pigs, sometimes for a song. And some of the eedjets think they're ruined."

" That's talk with skin on it," somebody said. " I know what I'm talkin' about," he said. " There isn't a man here who doesn't remember the time when a family in Aran, barrin' the police, the school teachers, the tax collector, the coastguards and other people like that, was lucky if a piece of mate was laid out on a table in it except around St. Martin's when a sheep, a goat or a cock was killed in honour of the Saint or at Christmas and on St. Patrick's Day, and it wasn't everybody could afford to kill a sheep on St. Martin's unless it was a sheep that was on its last legs, and if they didn't have somebody in America there were families that didn't see a bite of mate even at Christmas. I know what I'm talkin' about."

His audience nodded.

" Now, on me soul," he continued, " there's hardly a house you go into that hasn't a stripe of bacon hanging over the chimney, and where's the family that doesn't have a bit of fresh mutton once a week? I remember the time that a man would be afraid to fry a rasher for fear the shop-keeper that he owed money to would smell it and come around ballyraggin' him for atin' mate instead of paying his bills. They're atin' their own eggs, too, and hens no longer die of the weight of years. A woman now thinks no more of throwing a hen into a pot than she would of roasting a herring on the tongs."

He glanced round victoriously, leaned on his stick and waited for comment. Heads were nodded in approval. Even those who were hostile to De Valera were not hostile to meat.

Little Martin and I went up on deck. We were in sight of *Ceann Bóirne*, Black Head. Soon the islands would be in view. The boat was tossing in a heavy swell. There was little wind.

" What he is saying is true I hear," Little Martin said. " They tell me that every Saturday a string of fast ponies can be seen galloping towards Kilronan from every village in the island with a bag of mutton in front of every rider. You'd see more women going around there now getting customers for meat than you'd see gathering seaweed on the shore. Why, the young men of Gort na gCapall meet a couple of times a week in a house in the village and play cards for a sheep. I heard of a man who was so miserly that he went to bed with a broken heart when he came home one evening and found the small half of a bream roasting on the tongs. Now, that same man had to be taken to the hospital in Galway last week, with the boils breaking out all over his body from too much bacon he ate. You know the man I mean. He drew his money out of the bank and buried it under a flagstone near his house so it would be near him."

" Is he the man who used to eat guillemots on Friday with the excuse that they were fish because they never flew over land and lived on sea food? "

" The same man. How well you remember it! That used to be said by the old people and it is about the only thing in the way of knowledge that he ever learned. And he wouldn't bother learning that same only it was useful to him."

" And he's eating meat now? "

" Eating himself to death," he laughed. " Do

you remember the time we had the anti-treating pledge in Aran? "

" Yes. I used to serve at Mass when the stations came to our village Christmas and Easter."

" Do you remember the day the station was in the weaver's house and the priest was asking everybody if they kept the pledge? "

" I do."

" Well," laughed Little Martin, " when it came to this man's turn to speak he said that he kept the pledge, but if he knew that he couldn't take a drink from a neighbour he'd never take it and that it would be the last pledge of its kind he'd ever take. Now, when that kind of a man is killing himself with meat you must admit that a great change has come over the island."

" It is not a change," I said. " It is a revolution. I suppose the war had a lot to do with it. There was a lot of money made in Aran during the war."

" Money! You never saw as much money in your life, and you must have seen a lot of money in your travels. There was as much money made as would cover the islands with one-pound notes. Why, money was so plentiful that a man would not stoop down to pick up a ten-shilling note."

" I know a man who had his dog trained to go to the publichouse for a bottle of whiskey. He'd put a five-pound note in a pocket book and hang it on the dog's neck. The dog would come back with the bottle and the change! "

" How much of that money was saved? "

" It went as fast as it came. I know houses where as much as one hundred pounds came into it after a night's fishing. They hadn't as much as the price of a pound of tea a year after the war ended. People say money made on a war doesn't bring luck. Well, we're in sight of Inisheer." He pointed towards what looked like a blue cloud on the horizon.

" They say that at one time Galway Bay was a lake and that the Aran Islands were joined together, and to the County Clare on one side and Galway on the other. It is how the sea broke through. Maybe it is true and maybe it is not. How many acres of land in the three islands— or what we call land? "

" About eleven thousand I believe. What is the population now? There were about twenty-five hundred living on them when I left home."

" There wouldn't be that many now. Probably not more than two thousand or a little over.

" There were over thirty-five hundred in 1841. After that the famine began to do its work. And what the famine left, America took. But sure she's sending us back one or two good men anyhow."

I glowed at the caress of his voice.

"And there'll be a welcome before them?" I queried.

"*Mh'anam go mbeidh*—-My soul but there will," said he warmly, "and twenty welcomes."

A YOUNG MAN asked us in a London accent if the steamer was going direct to Aran or would she stop at the islands. She was going to Aran Mór first to catch the tide. He was sorry. He would like to see the curachs taking the cargo and live stock away from the *Dún Aonghus*. He was visiting Aran Mór for the first time as the guest of Robert J. Flaherty, the famous film director.

A man from the western end of Aran Mór who had joined us on deck, cocked his ears at the mention of Mr. Flaherty. He broke out in Gaelic :

" The O Flaherty "—that's his title in Aran until the end of time—" is the greatest man that ever came to Aran. If we had four more like him we'd never know a day's want. That's what everybody's saying. It would take five men like The O Flaherty to give enough work to the people so that nobody would be in need."

" Arrah, eternal bad condition on you, Tom Micheleen," said the lively old fellow of seventy with the game leg, " sure you know that it isn't work the wise people of Aran want. It's money they want."

The little man danced around his stick and gave such an excellent impersonation of a rooster among his hens that I would not be a bit surprised if he crowed!

Tom Micheleen turned his head to one side like a hen in the attitude of sneaking up on her nest.

" And isn't that what The O Flaherty is giving them? Money and no work or very little of it anyway."

" Ach," the agile philosopher of the simple life retorted : " Sure ye poor devils are so used to hard work that ye don't know what it is to do a day's work without killin' yourself. The O Flaherty is a civilized man and doesn't believe in making mules out of his men. But what every mother's son of ye wants is money and not work! Am I right or am I wrong? "

I confessed with apparent reluctance that I agreed with him.

" But," said Tom Micheleen, " how can you make money without working for it? "

The man with the stick snorted.

" Would you call work going around takin'

pictures? Or walking along the tops of the cliffs looking for a sun fish? Or galloping along the road on a horse with a straddle on him—that's not work—that's fun?"

"Well now," said Tom Micheleen, with a look of confusion on his face, "what you say would be true if they thought they were doing it for fun, but they think it is work."

"Work! Nonsense!" said the man with the game leg. "They go out with The O Flaherty's trammels and catch bollach and ate them and then get paid for catchin' them!"

"Arrah, what does he care if they ate all the bollach in the sea?" said Tom. "They say he'd rather one good picture of a curach in a breaker than all the bollach that were ever in Aran."

The game-legged man and Tom Micheleen continued to fight on both sides of the question. The Londoner asked me if I knew an Aran Islander by the name of Liam O Flaherty.

"He is a brother of mine," I answered, "or *vice versa*."

"Are you anything to Robert Flaherty?"

"Flaherty and O Flaherties trace their origin to he wilds of Conamara," I said. "The clan is dying out on the male side ; but it has provided wives for half Ireland ! "

We were passing Inisheer in the distance. Through a glass one could see a sandy shore and villages snuggling under cliffs. A deep valley ran in a south-westerly direction through the island.

" There is a lake in that island and its depth is not known," Little Martin said. " People say it would make the finest dry dock in the world."

Inismaan came into view. Bleak and bare it looked on this wintry day. People were gathered at the shore on the east side of the island ready to launch their curachs if the steamer decided to stop on her way to Aran Mór. Four villages nestled under cliffs. There is no police station on Inismaan. In my days a priest used to come from Aran Mór on Sundays to say Mass in Inismaan and Inisheer. Now there is a curate stationed on Inisheer. This is the only one of the islands where the Gaelic language is almost exclusively used. The natives can speak English, but they don't. From the point of view of business ability they are ahead of the people of the two other islands. They have consistently refused to pay either rates or taxes, and even in the days when landlords were in flower they did not pay enough rent to keep the landowner in tobacco. They are committed to the theory that they should be paid a bounty for living on the island and preserving the Gaelic language. And I'm thinking they're right.

The Inismaan fishermen follow their main source of livelihood all the year round, and they manage to find a market for their fish. In fact I was told that this was one of their best seasons.

Whether it is due to their refusal to be Anglicised or to the absence of Government authority in the island, the Inismaan folk are gayer than the people of the other two islands, freer from conventions, less bashful and more sociable. They visit freely in each other's homes and céilidhes are almost nightly affairs. As a result of this congenial atmosphere Inismaan is a byword among the sister islands for its simple and joyous life.

We pass Gregory's Sound that divides Inismaan from Aran. We turn by Straw Island in towards the little harbour of Kilronan. I am glad to be back again ; but I am sad also. For underneath the tombstones in the little churchyard on the sandy shore of Killeany lie the remains of many of those who bid me a tearful farewell when I left Kilronan pier twenty-one years ago!

I find my breath coming quicker. There is a queer dryness on my lips as the boat slows down and crawls the last few hundred yards. A jangling of bells, a stamping of feet, a shout from the shore and then at last with a bump and a grunt the *Dún Aonghus* ties up at the pier.

Without waiting for the gangway I leap the rail. I am home! Home in Aran!

Tom O'Flaherty

Born in 1889 on Inis Mór, the largest of the Aran Islands, Tom O'Flaherty showed a precocious scholastic ability from an early age. He also acquired an early concern for social and political change. His parents had been active in the Land League and were veterans of the pitched battles which took place between the islanders and the RIC during evictions. Tom and his younger brother, Liam, joined the Irish Volunteers, but in 1912 Tom emigrated, like many islanders before and after him, to the United States.

He settled in Boston, becoming an active member of the Socialist Party — then a party of some size and influence. After the Russian Revolution he joined John Reed and Jim Larkin in founding the American Communist Party and served on its Central Committee for many years. He put his considerable skills as a writer to work as a left-wing newspaper columnist, most notably in "As We See It" in the *Daily Worker*. He wrote often of the Easter Rising and the October Revolution and sought to draw a connection between them.

In 1919 he was visited by Liam, whom he

encouraged to take up writing. Later he moved to Chicago, where he became the first editor of the weekly *Voice of Labour*. In 1928, concerned at the degeneration of the Russian Revolution, he supported the Left Opposition and Leon Trotsky and joined James P. Cannon in setting up the Communist League of America.

Although most of his time and energy as a writer were devoted to the cause of political change, he also wrote short stories in both Irish and English. He returned to Ireland in 1934 to edit *An tÉireannach*, the weekly newspaper founded by poet Máirtín Ó Direáin, and in the same year *Aranmen All* was first published. Suffering from a weak heart, his health was too poor to let him take on the editorship of the paper, but he did contribute a substantial number of articles and short stories to it. Politically, he supported the non-Stalinist element of the left-wing Republican Congress. He spent eighteen months in Dublin and England, returning to Inis Mór in January 1936. His second book of short stories, *Cliffmen of the West*, was published that year. Worn out by illness, he died on the island on 10 May 1936 at the age of forty-seven.